*In Memory of Sapphire and Calvin.*
*Your lives were fleeting, beautiful*
*and glowing with a warmth which*
*forever changed everyone you touched.*

*You will always live within my heart and guide me.*

*Thank you, Louise*
*For your love and support x*

Divergent Mind Books

Published by Divergent Mind Books

Third paperback edition 2025

ISBN: 978-1-7394124-8-7

# The Miller's Apprentice

David Peters

Divergent Mind Books

# Chapter Index

# Life on Mantle

Carrying flour from the last mill on Mantle to the bakery owned by the miller's wife was back-breaking work, especially after a good rain the likes of which yesterday had seen! The ground was still muddy, and Kedrick had to watch his step as it was only too easy to slip on the wet streets of Kevlar, and slipping was never a good idea when you are carrying a heavy bag of flour on your back! Kedrick had paced these streets more than most, delivering flour to the Bakery and collecting wheat from the farmers' market and the storehouse building on the edge of town. He knew every pothole off by heart, which served him well in avoiding them on days like today, when an innocently shallow-looking puddle could be a pothole of ankle depth in disguise and so often was.

This is how his life had been since old Daisy passed on two months ago. She had been a faithful cart horse and, having helped the miller deliver his bags of flour for many years, old Daisy had been more of a family member than just a horse to the miller. Like so many of the livestock of Mantle, poor old Daisy had fallen ill drinking from that rotten River Qualm when both Kedrick, the miller's apprentice, and old Daisy had been on their way home from a long trip. No one had yet realised the dangers of that river, so Kedrick had let a very tired and thirsty Daisy take a rest and drink there. He regretted having stopped there later on that day when the poor old girl fell ill. That night, old Daisy had gone crazy and kicked her stable doors half off their hinges before starting to shake violently, and no amount of reassuring and calming words made a blind bit of difference for this poor, old horse. After a little more than an hour had passed, she dropped to the floor, slipping into semi-consciousness and remaining there for the night, breathing only shallow breaths. Kedrick and the miller had stayed at her side the whole night, praying for any sign of improvement. When the morning broke, as the first few rays of sunlight entered the stable and kissed old Daisy gently on the face, her whole body, which had been tensed up all night struggling for survival through the harsh cold temperatures, relaxed with the sun's warmth and she slowly slipped into total unconsciousness and then out of life into the peace of the afterlife. Her body was peaceful and still now.

A single tear rolled down the miller's face as he realised his longtime friendship had come to an end. He stood up, wiping the tears away and looking down at old Daisy. He turned briefly away towards Kedrick and said, "Make the arrangements for the old girl, Kedrick". "Do you want me to get farmer Tate to take her?", "TATE!! I'll not have Tate take her; there will be no mass grave for old Daisy, oh no, most definitely not!

Get Ted, he still has a sacrificial slab at his farm, and he owes me a favour from a while ago. Yes, get Ted!"

Ted's farm was half a day's walk on foot, so Kedrick set off right away. Normally, Kedrick was of the opinion that anything and everything didn't have any righteous claim on his time before he had eaten his breakfast, but this matter was different, especially as he felt somewhat to blame for poor old Daisy's demise! If only he hadn't stopped, he thought. But now that she was gone, the miller refused to buy another horse because he still blamed Kedrick for the plight of Daisy. The miller had grown quite attached to old Daisy over the years, so he had made Kedrick suffer these last couple of months by making him do all the carting about with the flour!

The Bakery was on the other side of town from the mill, and pushing the cart full of flour up the hill to the bakery was hard work, and it took Kedrick far longer than it would have taken old Daisy to do the run. The only lucky thing, as far as doing the run went, was that the amount of flour to deliver was dwindling each week as less and less corn and wheat came into the miller. Wheat just wasn't growing as well as it should be. So, currently, Kedrick found himself only needing to transport one bag of flour a day, so he just carried it on his back.

Kedrick was a handsome young Kevlarian man. People who knew his family often wondered where his good looks came from, as he was from very plain stock. He partially resembled his father, but with a certain something that added a great deal to the character of his face. "A throwback from an ancestor," Kedrick always told himself. In fact, sometimes he even dreamed about it, and as Sir Kedrick, he would order people about. The miller kept on telling Kedrick that one day, with hard work and dedication, he would make a fine miller and would be able to attract enough interest to be able to set up his own mill! The miller loved his job, and he believed that flour was the thing of the future, "Loaf!" he would say, "you don't get anything better than Loaf!" Of course, he was quite wrong; in fact, nine tenths of the population despised Loaf; they just couldn't fathom why anyone would eat such a plain-tasting food when there was such an abundance of fish to be had. Kedrick was more interested in his daydream adventures than in milling wheat. Crop farming was his first love; he loved the seasonal changes and everything about it, but at the moment, the miller's apprentice was as close as he could come to the job he wanted.

What made his job a little more bearable was the character of the miller. On the whole he was a cheerful soul, he never had a bad word to say about anyone and only really made Kedrick cart the heavy bags of flour about because secretly he couldn't afford to buy a new horse as business was too slow these days and for that reason, Kedrick thought, if he was to do anything with a business plan in mind it wouldn't involve anything agricultural until things improve. Currently, the best income is being gained by the fishermen as fish is the main diet of the people at the moment. Of course, at the present time, starting up a new fishing boat was quite costly; the price of anything fish-related had been increasing rapidly since crops had been failing, livestock falling ill and dying. As fish was the tastiest and nearly the only food source left, the demand for it had spiralled, along with taxes on fish sold and fishing permits. In addition, boat builders who had got in on the act by hiking their boat prices now found themselves being hit by a large tax bill on every sale. So, despite the temptation to become a fisherman, the truth was that their personal income wasn't that much more than before.

At one time, the wheat crops had flourished and Loaf was very popular, almost a gift from the gods, but the earth had undergone changes; the wheat had started to taste different; it now had a metallic taste about it, and the crops were harvested less and less. The once-thriving Loaf industry had died, and now there was only one miller left. Business was hard, and he could only use a quarter of the wheat that his farming colleagues harvested, as they had to use three-quarters of the wheat to re-plant for the next harvest. Each season, they were harvesting less and less, and many had packed in farming and taken up fishing; others soldiered on thanks purely to the miller's subsidies. In fact, he was presently taking in such a small amount of wheat and was subsiding the farmers' losses to such an extent that he was not turning any profit at all and could barely pay for the upkeep of the mill (parts of the mill were currently unusable due to the leaks in the roof, but as the mill was not running on full capacity it didn't really matter). Soon, if things did not change, the miller would have to close the mill or call on his wife's business to bail him out, as he had spent all of his savings on subsidising the farmers. But for now, he could carry on and just agonise about what he would do next month!

Most people, including his farming colleagues, simply thought that the miller had suffered some kind of nervous breakdown and was trying to clutch on to the straws of a previous life, when life had been good. However, the truth of the matter was that the miller was intolerably stubborn; he refused to believe that the Loaf industry was really dead and was just putting off the inevitable. He envisioned that the harvest would again become plentiful, that the popularity of Loaf would rise and that he would be the only miller and therefore make a fortune, maybe having a string of mills across the country. Ever the optimist, this thought reigned supreme in the miller's head and pushed back his concerns over next month's payments to a long-forgotten corner of his mind, allowing his broad, beaming smile to return again to his face along with calmness to his previous unsettled thoughts. Life in Kevlar was generally peaceful, at least most of the time, and that is how the miller liked it.

Occasional fits of mass depression would hit the village when the rains came from the north and the east. No one knew why this was, but the Council of the Elders, who met every day, but officially once a week, always blamed the great wizard Asthal, who now lived past the forest of Xendar.

"Why would a great wizard like Asthal be content in making people in his old village depressed?" thought Kedrick. He had said as much to the Elders in the past, but they refused to believe that Asthal was not the cause of the problem. Kedrick had vowed to find out the truth for himself one day, but as time went on, Kedrick had forgotten this promise that he had made to himself.

The Council of the Elders had asked Asthal to leave the village about ten years ago due to an incident that had distressed many of the village folk, and that the Elders had, as usual, been quick to pin the blame on the wise old wizard. You see, the people of Kevlar used to be obsessed with hats, although the term hats barely covers the obsession they once had. All kinds of headgear used to be worn. One trend that sent people running out of their homes to buy a new hat was the Dough Cap. Believe it or not, the Dough Cap became popular during a hot summer month and was literally a cap of dough, a half-baked Loaf in the shape of a cap! People bought it in their droves, and with the unusual heat wave they were having, the dough would slowly bake on their heads, giving off the smell of baking bread wherever they went! The Kevlarian's went mad for it, and production could barely keep on top of demand. The miller was in his element; he thought everyone was stark raving mad for wearing Loaf on their heads and was saddened that so little of his product would actually be eaten, as Loaf that had been sat upon someone's head all day was not something you would want to eat! But he was happy to be so busy milling every ounce of flour that he could, and seeing a big smile on his wife's face gave him a warm feeling too, as his wife, who owned the Bakery, making the stupid Dough Caps, was making a fortune.

All was well, at least that was until heavy rains came following the unusual heat wave and the Kevlarian's found soggy sticky dough oozing down their faces and necks. It was a bad day for the miller's wife as she had customer after customer demanding their money back for the ruined produce! It didn't harm her business as she had made so much money from the Dough Caps already over the past two weeks, but to hit such a sudden drop in sales, along with the day of complaints, affected her and she fell into a month-long depression.

It broke the miller's heart to see her so glum. He kept trying to pep her up by coming up with new sales ideas, like a Loaf that had jam in it or a Pie that had two parts, one with a meat stew in and one with custard and fruit in, a meal and pudding in one. But no matter what he suggested, his wife didn't cheer up until the end of the month, when the accounts had to be done, and she slowly started the task with a long face. By the time the miller popped in to try again to cheer his wife up during lunch, she was a completely different woman, gone was the tired, sad and lonely woman the miller had suffered with for the last month and back was the happy and excited businesswoman that he loved so much. "Do you know that we made twice the amount selling Dough Caps that we would have made selling the same amount of plain loaf!" she exclaimed, "This is really something here, we need more adventurous ideas! What was that idea you said? Jam in Loaf? We will try it tomorrow!", she said leaving the miller stood in the office of her Bakery as she went to the ovens where her staff had the afternoons supply of Loaf cooking and told them of her plan to put jam into some of the Loaves tomorrow! The miller didn't mind that he had been left on his own; he liked his own company anyway, and he was so happy to see his wife smiling again, and to actually like one of his suggestions was just the cherry on the cake.

This sogginess of caps malarkey was not enough to deter the hat culture in Kevlar. The next day, there was a new hat to go crazy over. And so, it went on until that day, the blackest day in the history of Kevlar.

The day that the people now would not even mention, as it was too painful a memory for them, and it was all thanks to Asthal, or at least that is what the Council of the Elders led everyone except Kedrick to believe.

The truth of the matter was, of course, that Asthal did not have a hand in this grave matter. However, there was a young apprentice working under the wizard and in his private studies he had come across an old spell that he thought would improve the nation's health and being a true ultramist (which is an extreme optimist) he decided that he should perform this task, the task of reading the spell out loud, an incantation to help the nation he loved so much. Unfortunately, being an apprentice and a novice at wizardry, he did not realise that such vague spells should never be used despite the repeated warnings from his mentor. "Specifics, specifics, specifics", Asthal would teach, but Grundlenut, his apprentice obviously didn't pay any heed as one night whilst the wizard slept, he conjured the dubious spell with ceremonious pride, wearing his best wizardry clothes,"Gehernum Di Albun, Ki slarun, Gelauf!", he chanted repeatedly half expecting some great sign from mother nature that the spell had worked and all was well, or very well in the case of this spell, but nothing happened at all and Grundlenut felt rather disappointed with this anticlimax and went to bed with his mind set on giving up on magic the next day.

The next day came, and the early rays of sunlight flickered beautifully across the country, gradually stirring every creature into wakefulness, and when the Kevlarians awoke, all that was heard was screaming followed by sobbing. Their hats, it would seem, had turned into hat-shaped croaking frogs that constantly broke wind. It seemed that through magical genius, the spell figured out exactly what was bad for Kevlar, and that was the people's obsession with hats and found a completely novel way to disrupt that infatuation! The people did not know why they were so attached to wearing their big, bright, and colourful hats; that painful knowledge had been long forgotten, buried deep in the back of the minds of their ancestors. The hats, of course, were one of the last traits that still held a place in their culture, in the same way that they did 347 years ago. When the last Veneficus (as they were called) lay down his rare and prestigious wand that had been crafted from the Tusk of an ancient Gregal.

Visually, the Gregal was an imposing sight, a shaggy mountain of an animal, very much similar to that of our woolly mammoths, dwarfing modern elephants. Its most striking feature was its incredibly thick coat, a dense two-layered affair: a fine, insulating underfur of light brown or reddish-brown, and long, coarse hairs, perhaps up to a meter in length, that could range from dark brown to black, giving it a somewhat grizzled, almost muddy appearance in places. These long hairs hung down, sometimes obscuring its legs and belly, creating a powerful silhouette. Aurally, the Gregal was a creature of low, rumbling sounds. A deep, resonant bellows that vibrated through the air and ground of the central plains. Whilst the air around them would carry a potent, earthy scent as the smell of damp, coarse fur mingled with the faint musk of a large animal. Sadly, these magnificent creatures are very much confined to the history books, just like our woolly mammoths. There was, however, one small characteristic which very much set the Gregal apart from our mammoths. The Gregal could float up to five feet off the ground with very little effort at all. How these amazing beasts attained this apparently magical ability was never known. Many academics have since formulated theories on the very subject, trying to get to the root of the matter. Of the many opinions and theories put forth, two camps of belief existed. Some felt the beasts were naturally buoyant creatures, attributing such buoyancy to a float bladder, where digestive gases would be held, making the creatures lighter than air itself! This camp was rather logical and considered the physics of the matter, creating a float bladder filled with hydrogen gas to enable said floating. Now, such a chamber inside the creature would surely have been very uncomfortable, not to mention disastrous if they broke wind anywhere near a naked flame! No, it is certainly the second camp that hit the nail on the head with their theory of magical inference. They felt the Gregal gained their magical ability via their choice of grazing sites, which, according to historical records, ran mostly along the central lines of magic. These are heavily documented pathways of Mantle. One unresolved issue with this theory is whether the animals chose to use their ingested power to float or whether this was just a side effect! Sadly, the creatures became an extinct species around 800T.P., which ties in with a downturn in the levels of magic flowing across the Mantle at the time. It was put forth, and still is commonly thought, that the digestive systems of the Gregal had become over-reliant on the magical element in their diet, and the sudden downturn in magic didn't give the animals sufficient time to adapt and evolve into less magical creatures, so they perished. The real reason, on the other hand, had nothing to do with struggling digestive systems but simply that without the ability to float, these poor creatures simply lost their lust for life. Faced with a future of simply trudging about on all fours, eating non-magical grass, they despaired and went on a hunger strike that wiped out the entire population.

The old hats of the Veneficus (or Wizards) would stand tall and proud, majestic, with a slightly lopsided cone that seemed to defy gravity. Their primary colour was a deep, faded sapphire blue, almost bordering on indigo, a testament to countless moonlit nights spent studying the art of magic. They told everything about the old wizards, such as how many years they had been practising and even what their wand was made from. But most importantly, it was how they ranked themselves in the hierarchy of their wizarding society, for the more ornate a hat, the higher the wizard stood in their magical society.

Some Kevlarians, being quite determined, wore their altered hats for the first week before they, too, finally broke down in streams of tears. If that was not bad enough, many people had gone out to buy new hats that had freshly been made on that first day, only to find that whilst they slept that night, the same thing happened to these new hats. All in all, one spell forever banished hats from Kevlar.

Consequently, a meeting of the Elders was held on behalf of the people, and as the problem was quite clearly magical, Asthal caught the blame. Even the pleading and confession of his apprentice fell on deaf ears, and he was asked to leave, asked, mind you, not ordered or banished, for you see the Elders were quite fearful of what the wizard could do to them if he so chose. But he was a peaceful man and couldn't much abide the majority of the villagers anyway, so he just left muttering something to himself about specifics being the first lore of wizardry, and that was that.

Kedrick hadn't always been a miller's apprentice; he used to work in the farming fields of the now Thurk Nation, before they had declared self-rule of their district. You see, when working in the farming fields there, the quiet farming town of Thurk was a lovely place, quite peaceful with a large town square that hosted the farmers' market every Thursday. This was the only time the peace and quiet of the town was disturbed, by boisterous farmers selling their wares, noisy, smelly cattle, sheep, and fowl playing their part in the hectic day of the farmers' market. All in all, life was good back then. Kedrick loved farming, the sowing of the crops every spring, the harvesting every summer and autumn, and even the winter preparation warmed his heart on cold winter days. He thought he had truly found his place in the world, back then, farming!

But life changed as it always does, the blight struck the lands east of the River Qualm and crops failed time and time again, even the crops far down past the great city of Targon started to fail, leaving the fields of Thurk the main resource of the great nations of Mantle. The town then grew and grew, becoming noisier and more hectic each week. Great buildings were erected around the town as the wealth of the residents grew. The mayor of the town's ego also grew along with the town's popularity. Then, in response to thieves' attempts to steal from the farmer's warehouse the night before market day, Mayor Thump declared that a large wall be built, closing the Town of Thurk off from the nations of Mantle, purely to protect their valuable crops.

As time went on, eventually the townsfolk too became big-headed about their town's worth, and it was put forward that they should form their own nation. By this time, young Kedrick was losing interest in the new idea of farming that was being forced upon him by the rich farmers, who were getting richer and richer.

For years, they had grown the best and the tastiest fruit and vegetables by using natural ways of enriching the land. If an animal died, after cutting away all useful meat and processing it, they would leave the animals unwanted bones on a sacrificial slab of rock which they had in the farms main yard near the compost pile and by morning the bones would have vanished and in their place, there would be a pile of rich compost that they then added into their own compost heap.

Kedrick had often wondered what happened overnight to the bones; no one knew because the reason why they performed the ritual of bone sacrifice had been lost. They thought they did it to avoid being cursed, but that wasn't the truth of the matter. So, one night, Kedrick had lain in wait to see what happened; he had asked others to come with him, but all were too afraid, and when he had told them of his plans, they all said goodbye to him as if he would never return. Superstition ran high in Thurk, and they expected any sort of meddling with the old rituals would result in a loss of life.

As Kedrick waited, a group of bats flew overhead, and he recognised the bats; they were from Xendar Forest. Kedrick remembered seeing them flying about the forest late one evening when he had been hunting with his father as a young man of seventeen. They landed around the bones and sniffed the air around the bones. Then, in one uniform movement, they all opened their mouths to expose razor-sharp teeth and together started eating the bones in a frenzy. It took only two minutes for them to completely reduce the bones of the cow to nothing but the compost that the bats' own digestive processes had created. Of course, when Kedrick told his friends the following day, they said that just because he was too scared to keep a vigil on the cow's bones last night, he didn't have to make something up and laughed at him! Of course, Kedrick knew the truth of the matter. But that was a long time ago, and under the new rules, everything had changed. They had stopped sacrificing animal bones after scares that the dying cattle were infected with some kind of illness, as many animals who had drank from the River Qualm had not long after died, and due to the large numbers of animals dying, the farmers decided the best option was to dig deep ditches for the dead animals and set fire to them. Kedrick had witnessed one such painful event firsthand; he had witnessed how the air grew thick with the acrid stench of burning flesh and hair, which shimmered above the pit as guttural crackle and the roar of the flames consumed the piled forms, casting an infernal flickering glow.  Then later, they had filled the ditch in with soil and rock, preventing the Mireal Bats from getting the food they needed so much.

Up and down the country, sacrificial slabs were broken up and used as rock to fill ditches. And that wasn't the only change; farmers wanted to produce more with less, so dangerous cocktails were made up to increase the production of the crops! In some instances, they worked with no noticeable side effects; vegetables grew twice as big as did the fruit. In other instances, the crops withered and died off. But even when the cocktails worked, the resulting produce, although bigger, tasted bland in comparison to the old produce.

Kedrick didn't like the new ways and had left the farms of Thurk behind in search of new work. He had been brought up on Thurk, and leaving the now nation of Thurk pulled heavily on his mind; he didn't really want to leave, but knew he couldn't stay because the new ways aggravated him too much. So, he set off to the next village to try and find work on a farm, but the village was Un-Nuk, and they had no farms and sent the young man on to Kevlar, telling him that they had fields, farms, and even a mill. So, he tried the fields of Kevlar for work, but there was no need for any extra farm workers due to the poor crops they now kept getting. So, moving on to the village of Kevlar, his continued search for work found him talking to the miller and appreciative of young Kedrick's honest effort to find work, he felt he must help him and created the role of miller's apprentice for Kedrick to fulfil.

# The Mireal Bat

With the dietary requirements of the Mireal bat going unmet, the poor creatures started to die off in their droves. A few of the more intelligent bats realised that if they did not want to become documented victims of an interrupted food chain, they would have to start looking elsewhere for nourishment. They guided the less mentally endowed of their group to join them in this endeavour, and it was a huge culture shock for them, because for hundreds of years they had quite happily had their food put out on a plate for them, so to speak, and now they had to hunt!

To say the least, they did not take to their new lives like ducks to water! In fact, I think a far more accurate analogy would be like fish to sand. They sucked at it, and many of them still perished. Desperate to survive and find a new source of food, the Mireal bats would venture out of the evening, out of the Forest and out of the countryside that had been their whole world for so long, and into the bright noisiness of the city!

The bravest of the bats led the way; at a good seventy feet above the ground, he performed a high-level aerial recon of the city with four other bats following him, in tight formation. Their long, purposeful noses, for once, were performing the job they were designed by nature to carry out; they were sniffing, sniffing for food, or bone-like substances, to be more specific. On their first pass, nothing came up on their radar. "Maybe there simply was no food for them here", the brave lead bat thought, or perhaps they had been just flying too high! So, they dropped their altitude to fifty feet above the ground and swung around for a second run over the city. As they neared the halfway point, they had again found nothing, but then the bat at the rear left of their squadron smelled a scent that drove his senses crazy; it was a faint scent, but it was sweet. Aware of his discovery, the other bats soon picked up the scent and followed it stealthily to its source in the backyard of a building. It was coming out of the ground, and the bats had to use their feet to dig out what the rain had buried earlier that evening: Teeth! Or more importantly, young teeth. Teeth from a young animal tasted to a Mireal bat like honey does to you and me. They tucked into their treasure quickly like the hungry bats they were, but then something disturbed them; a man opened the back door to the building and threw something at them. The bats, completely startled by this, flew off as quickly as they could, like crows that had been shooed by a farmer, later reporting their findings to their elderly Chief on their return to the main camp.

His decision was that they wait a couple of hours until no one is stirring in the city. Then, they would each take it in turn, in groups of four, to visit this backyard of teeth. The weaker and hungrier bats would feed first.

And so they did until not a single tooth was left within reach of their feet.

The next morning, the man occupying that building woke up quite early and made himself breakfast, before opening time, as usual. Whilst he was drinking his morning cup of Tea, he remembered the fright he had been given when he had opened the back door last night! So, he happened to look out of his back window and couldn't believe his eyes. he didn't know what had happened last night, but all the ground in his backyard had been completely turned over, and not a single tooth was visible on the surface anywhere! Was this a blessing, maybe, he wondered, as he hadn't quite known what to do with all the teeth he had!

You see, this was the home and business of Dr Henry, a Dental Practitioner. As Targon City had no refuge collection or teeth removal service, Dr Henry had just been throwing each day's extracted teeth onto the ground of his backyard. He knew it wasn't ideal, but he didn't know what else to do with them! But now, they had all gone.

As the day passed for Dr Henry, he pulled more teeth out and, at the same time, contemplated many times what had gone on last night. His main customers were the elderly, whose teeth had rotted away to nothing and children, whose milk teeth had got wobbly and were causing them pain. Most parents wouldn't or couldn't pay for their children's milk teeth to be extracted, so Dr Henry never charged to treat children, as he didn't like the thought of the poor things suffering. But the elderly he charged, because he had to spend a long time digging out broken bits of old rotten teeth on a regular basis with the elderly customers he had, and despite their age and meagre income, he felt he should be compensated for the time he put in, but still didn't charge full price.

For this reason, he was quite popular with the children and elderly patients; in fact, he mainly only had children and elderly patients on his books and was well on his way to going bankrupt thanks to his poor business sense!

As the day drew to a close, Dr Henry locked his front door and wondered what he should do with the twelve teeth he had extracted during the day! He walked over to the back door with the jar of teeth in his hand, opened the door, and threw the teeth onto the ground. It hadn't rained at all today, the ground was dry, and they sat proudly on the surface. Dr Henry sat down on the back doorstep and waited and waited.
Nothing happened. He waited longer still, until darkness started to creep over the city as nightfall came. He lit a candle and waited longer again.

After an hour, the Mireal bats flew into Dr Henry's backyard and landed on the ground where the teeth had been thrown. As they picked the teeth up in their clawed feet, they noticed Dr Henry just sitting there, not moving, just watching them. They paused for a moment, ready to flee, and then relaxed and used their small claw-like hands to pick the teeth up properly and ate them, excreting compost-like poop as they consumed the food. Each of the five bats ate one tooth and then flew away. Still, Dr Henry waited to see what would happen to the remaining seven teeth. He didn't have to wait long, as the bats had told the group of the seven teeth remaining and of the watchful man, so seven bats carefully entered the back yard and started to nibble gingerly at the remaining teeth as, again, the man watched on. As soon as the bats had eaten all the teeth, they flew off, and the man, bewildered by them, went inside and had his dinner! He smiled to himself as he had dinner, "Little teeth tidier's!" he said to himself and chuckled.

This occurrence repeated itself every day, and the dentist and the bats grew used to each other. Eventually, another problem presented itself to the good Dr; the bat poop was starting to pile up a bit, and if this relationship he had with the Bats was to continue, he would have to think of a way to remove the poop! The answer came from yet another accident of nature, a bird must have, whilst flying directly over the Dr's backyard, subconsciously decided to sow a tomato plant seed in the pile of poop from the bats. Within a week, a tomato plant had grown, and within a month, it was fruiting. A fortnight later, the fruit was round, red and plump. The Dr who had been keeping an eye on the tomato plant picked the juiciest-looking tomato and bit into it; a sudden gush of flavour lapped around the Dr.'s mouth and with a swallow sank down to his stomach! The dentist was very pleased, "Now my little teeth tidier's are feeding me!" he laughed to himself. It had been a long time since he had tasted a tomato that actually tasted like one should, and then it hit him, it's compost, amazing compost, "I could sell compost, Dr Henry's Amazing Compost!" he said out loud to himself. He wondered if it was right to sell the bats' poop; after all, it relied on the bats' help to be able to do so. He knew the bats listened to him, but he didn't know if they understood him, as they always just looked at him when he talked, and never responded in any way.

That night, he spoke to them again, "If I continue to give you these teeth, will you be kind enough to leave me the compost that you have been doing, so that I might sell it to the farmers?" The bats looked at each other, and then one bat came forward from the rear. He wasn't the largest bat, nor the loudest, but his presence carried with it a palpable weight and a silent hum of authority resonated through the clustered, velvety forms of his kin as they moved aside, bowing their heads in respect. His fur, once a vibrant russet, was now a faded, mottled umber, softened by countless seasons and the gentle abrasion of rock and air. Around his shoulders, where the delicate bones of his wings met his body, there was a faint sheen, like worn velvet. His face was a tapestry of fine lines around eyes that, even in the dimmest light, held an ancient, knowing glint. They weren't just black beads; they were deep pools, reflecting the faint light of the house, hinting at centuries of watchful vigilance. His ears, oversized and almost translucent, were constantly twitching, like antennae sifting through the aural landscape surrounding him. You could almost feel the minute vibrations of the air as he processed the distant rustle of a beetle, the soft sigh of a draft, or the subtle shift in the flocks' murmur. One of his leathery wings, perhaps from an old skirmish or a particularly close call with a predator, bore a small, crescent-shaped tear near the trailing edge, a silent testament to battles fought and survived. As he shifted, moving towards the front of the flock, a faint, dry rustle emanated from his wings, like dead leaves skittering across stone. And if you listened more intensely, past the ceaseless, high-pitched chatter of the younger bats, you might catch the faintest, almost imperceptible purr deep in his chest; a vibration of contentment, perhaps, or merely the slow, steady rhythm of a life lived long and wisely. Once standing at the front of the party of bats, he raised his head to look at the dentist and gave a solitary nod, then returned to his original post, and the night's feast resumed.

The next day, after buying a permit from the mayor's office, the dentist placed handmade posters around the city saying, "Farmers, get your crops to prosper, buy Dr. Henry's Amazing Compost!"

It wasn't too long before the Dentist was getting orders coming in from all over the nation, and he realised that he couldn't meet the demand with the number of extractions he made. He thought long and hard about what to do. For the dentist, it felt like a fantastic opportunity had presented itself and was about to slip through his fingers with the mounting pressure to fill orders that he was under.

Eventually, an idea popped into his mind and once more, he stepped out at night and spoke honestly to the bats, "I cannot meet the demand of the farmers for your special compost as things stand! But I have thought of a way that I can, with your help. If you are willing to help!", the elder bat again came from the rear to listen to what the dentist was going to ask of them, the dentist paid respect to the elderly bat by bowing his head slightly whilst maintaining eye contact, "Thank you for your attention", Dr Henry began, "I was thinking that if I mention to the children that come here, that when a tooth falls out they must put it on their window sill for the magical tooth fairy to take away. Then in exchange for them, you would leave a coin, and, if it works, it would, in time, yield a lot of teeth for you!" The bat looked bewildered at the man, his wise old eyes asking, 'How are we to pay for the teeth?' "Of course, I will leave a pile of coins in the back here for you to leave in place of the teeth! I think it will catch on with the children!" The worried look in the eyes of the old bat went away as his bewilderment was cured with the dentist's answer. He paused for a moment and looked about the cluster of bats as he considered whether this would be beneficial to his colony, then he turned back to the dentist and again gave one solitary nod and there, right at that moment, the Tooth Fairy was born.

The next night, the colony turned up at Dr Henry's, and each one took a coin from the pile and flew up and down each damp, cold street of the city sniffing for teeth with their purpose-made noses. Each unseen gust of wind carried the damp, metallic tang of rain-washed iron and a distant, almost imperceptible whisper of the forest. The air hung heavy, a biting chill that sank into the bones of the bats, despite their fur. Dim lights from the houses hummed a flickering, melancholic tune, casting elongated, shivering shadows that danced with phantom footsteps almost to the beat of the soft, rhythmic dripping from overflowing gutters. Only two teeth were found on that first night, and they returned largely unsatisfied to the dentists for their nightly feast.

The Next night, news had spread amongst the children of the tooth fairy, and more children left teeth out for them to take.

Within a month, Dr Henry realised he needed to move as the teeth were coming in so fast that they had started to pile up. Now, previously, only a handful of the bats were getting fed, but with Dr Henry's new scheme, each night that passed, more and more bats appeared, until through this process, he had started, all the Mireal bats of Mantle were getting fed each night.

To address this new challenge, the good doctor bought a piece of land in the middle of the forest where no one ever went. On the drive, he paid for large signs to be erected for his compost business, which was also going from strength to strength. In the back, he hid huge containers to hold the teeth until they were needed. He was set for life, and the Mireal bats had a purpose and a good diet. Everyone was happy.

# The Princess Kidnap

At the moment, life was far from peaceful as everyone was preparing for the visit of the young Princess Miasia, from the city of Targon. Her visit was in one week's time and everyone was rushing about making preparations; Mrs. Stew was making delicious fruit pies and tarts with surrounding crown edges, Mr. Rhodes was busy, sweeping the dry, dusty streets and cursing about dropped litter and even Kedrick's Grandma was busy making repairs to the flag of Targon, that was to be hoisted above the gates of the village. It was in a terrible state, having been cradled in the musty embrace of a forgotten attic, lying dormant since the last royal visit some five years ago. The air, thick with the scent of aged fabric and forgotten things, seemed to cling to the material, carrying with it the faint, sharp tang of mildew, which would have to be beaten out. It would appear that a Glock fly had flown into the box as the flag was packed away after the last visit and had survived the first couple of months of incarceration by nibbling on the crest of Targon before finally dying of boredom.

The jolly mayor of the village was having the most fun, running about shouting commands to each and every person he came across as fast as his chubby, little legs could carry him, "Lift that banner higher"," don't let it sag in the middle" he ordered, as the sweat of desperation ran down his forehead, which he wiped away with a white silk handkerchief he was holding in his podgy little right hand. The mayor was rattled by the suddenly announced visit, and a mild panic was going on under the normally calm outer surface. "These royal visits always come round too quickly, there's just not enough time to get everything ready, oh no, we're not going to be ready in time! One week is not enough! - Now hang on, get a hold of yourself, we will succeed", and that's what he kept telling himself.

The day of the visit finally arrived, and all of Kevlar crowded around the main entrance to the village, hoping for a glimpse of the Princess. Even young Toadleg and his friends were there. He had climbed an Elkberry Tree to try and get a better look. Toadleg was the first to spot the royal carriage arriving, "Here comes the Princess", he shouted. The crowd let out a giant cheer for the Princess.

But something was wrong; the carriage was travelling too fast. Sourced from some unseen terror, the carriage careened through the sun-baked streets, a phantom limb of a forgotten will. The air, already thick with the scent of parched earth and distant, shimmering heat, was now lacerated by the rhythmic, frantic clatter of hooves on stone. Two horses, magnificent beasts of a deep chestnut, were yoked to this runaway terror, their muscles bunching and releasing in a desperate, uncoordinated dance. Their eyes, usually placid pools reflecting the world at ease, were now wide and rolling, the whites stark against their dark coats. Fear, raw and unbridled, was etched into every trembling line of their powerful bodies. Their flanks, once smooth and glossy, were now lathered with a frothing, almost iridescent sweat, streaking down their glistening sides in rivulets that quickly picked up the pervasive dust, transforming the slickness into a gritty, streaky paste. They exulted the sharp, animal tang of exertion and pure terror, a scent that pricked the nostrils and spoke of desperation, now mingled with the dry, earthy smell of the road. They sped past the crowd and into the village, "It's not stopping!" shouted Eldark the Blacksmith, "It's a runaway", answered Alto, the eldest of the Elders. Longthorn set off on his horse to retrieve the carriage.

Moments later, the wounded remains of the Royal escort arrived. The first hint of their presence wasn't the fanfare of trumpets, but a low guttural murmur that rippled through the gathered townsfolk, a stark contrast to previous visits. Through the shimmering heat haze that clung to the cobblestones, they appeared. This was no triumphant event, but a limping, shattered remnant of what had once been a magnificent retinue. The sun, usually a warm embrace in late July, seemed to mock their broken state, highlighting every tear in their once-proud tunics, every splash of grim, dark stain against the faded livery. Horses, their heads bowed low, clip-clopped with an agonising slowness, some limping badly, their coats matted with dust and dried sweat. One, a magnificent grey warhorse, stumbled, and a collective gasp rose from the onlookers as a rider, his arm hanging at an unnatural angle, swayed precariously in the saddle before a comrade reached out to steady him. The air, usually scented with baking bread and fresh fish from the nearby market, was now thick with the metallic tang of blood and the acrid sting of fear. Faces, once etched with the confidence of royal service, were now drawn and pale, pained and exhausted. Their eyes, hollow and distant, scanned the crowd not with arrogance, but with a desperate plea for succour. Some clutched at makeshift bandages, their teeth gritted against the pain that radiated from unseen wounds. One young squire, no more than a boy, was slumped over the neck of his pony, his breathing shallow and ragged, a visual testament to the brutal encounter they had endured.

"The Princess has been kidnapped!" exclaimed the captain of the Royal Guard, who seemed to be the only man unscathed and with energy enough to carry on. "We were ambushed by servants of the uprising on our passage through the woods. My men are injured and need immediate attention. Arrange for them to be treated and gather a group of your finest men to go after the Princess", the captain instructed Alto. The village womenfolk took care of the injured whilst the captain and Alto selected some recruits from the gathering of volunteers that were all mad keen on rescuing a princess in her hour of need! Kedrick was the first in line, "I will go after the Princess, I am strong and quick and can fight as well as the next man" Alto looked to Kedrick's left, where Jim Dobb stood as still as he could. It was a kind of stillness which made everyone around him feel they were on a boat, the kind of stillness only a drunken fool can maintain. Don't get me wrong, Jim Dobb was a very nice fellow, it's just sobriety had never been his thing, and too many years of drinking had addled his brain. In fact, the only reason Jim was there at all was because he had mistaken the gathering for the queue that always occurred at the afternoon opening of the Tavern. "This is true, Kedrick, but you are also young and lacking experience of battle!" replied Alto. "This is my chance to experience battle!" rebutted Kedrick. "A fine choice," interrupted the captain. "We need five more men. Has anyone got any experience of Battle?" Bill Bracket stepped forward. "I served in the war against the uprising five years ago in Her Majesty Queen Dubark's Army.", "So did I", said Thark, the Tavern owner.

Gradually, a group of men were selected, and they stood in front of the captain. The sun beat down with an oppressive, blistering heat, turning Captain Blade's surcoat into a heavy, suffocating shroud. Dust, fine as flour, coated everything, clinging to his sweat-dampened skin. He had stood, like a solitary, unbowed oak amidst the splintered wreckage of his guard, and the air was still fresh and thick with the coppery scent of their blood.

Some had fallen, others were broken, their armour rent, but the captain, by some divine grace and years of honed skill, had remained unscathed. His gauntlets, though scuffed, showed no nicks, his helm bore no dent, a chilling testament to his mastery of blade and sword. His gaze, usually a sharp, commanding glint, was now a shimmering haze of grief and fierce resolve. He could still hear the princess's fading cries, a phantom echo that twisted his gut. His hands, calloused from countless drills and brutal skirmishes, clenched and unclenched at his sides, itching for the hilt of his sword. Now, as he turned, his eyes swept over the huddled townsfolk who had volunteered, their faces a mix of fear and clumsy determination. These were the blacksmiths, the bakers, the farmers, men whose hands were more accustomed to tools than weapons. A bitter taste, like ash, filled his mouth. This was his new guard, a desperate, ragtag posse replacing the disciplined warriors he had lost. He drew a ragged breath, the hot dusty air burning his lungs. The weight of his oath, of his failure, pressed down on him, a crushing burden. Yet, beneath the grief, a spark of defiance flickered, then roared into a blaze. The princess would be rescued. His guard would be avenged. And he, Captain Blade, would lead these raw recruits into the teeth of danger, forging them into the instruments of salvation. He would make them warriors, or he would die trying. The fate of the princess now rested on his solitary, skilled shoulders, and the courage he could ignite in the hearts

of these ordinary men. "Look around you!" The
captain's voice, though hoarse from battle, cut through
the oppressive stillness like a blade. "Look at your town,
silent and shadowed! It was not here, within these walls,
that my men fell. It was Robbers' Lane, a short distance
from here, where we were ambushed. They fell
defending what is ours, defending our Princess. And for
their courage, for their sacrifice, they deserve more than
just our sorrow." He paused, letting his gaze sweep over
each nervous face. "The curs who did this," he
continued, his voice hardening, "they fled north,
thinking themselves safe, thinking they've won. But they
haven't. Not whilst any single one of us still draws
breath! They have taken our Princess, a beacon of hope
for this kingdom, and they have butchered my loyal
guard. Do you think we stand idle? Do you watch as our
future is dragged into darkness?" The captain's hand
instinctively went to the hilt of his sword, a familiar
comfort in the chaos. "You are not soldiers," he
admitted, his voice softening slightly, yet still carrying
the weight of command. "Not yet. But you are fathers,
brothers, sons. You are the heart of this town. And
today, you are the last hope for our Princess. Every step
we take north, past Robber's Lane, will be a step
towards vengeance, a step towards salvation. We will
make those villains regret the day they ever set foot on
our soil!" His eyes blazed with an unshakeable resolve.
"Fear is a heavy burden, I know. But the shame of
inaction, the thought of what might become of our

Princess if we do nothing, that is a far heavier weight to bear. We ride north! We ride for our fallen comrades! We ride for our Princess! And by the heavens above, we will not return until she is safe, and those who have wronged us have paid in full!" He raised his hand, pointing northwards, towards the shimmering horizon. "Now, take up your arms! Look to the man beside you! Your lives depend on each other. Let us show these raiders the true might of this kingdom, the unwavering spirit of its people! For the Princess! For the Fallen! For the kingdom!" And with that, the captain pressed his heels into the flank of his horse, spurring it into motion, with the newly assembled rescue party, following suit and setting off after the Princess and after a battle!

None knew what would lie in store for them, and all felt the spirit riding with them in their veins, making their hearts beat faster, preparing them, making them stronger for battle. The lane was overgrown and had many bends, but blindly they charged on at full pace.

They journeyed to the point of the attack; it wasn't hard for them to miss as freshly splintered wood and fallen soldiers covered the ground. It was clear by looking at the fallen that the attack had been fast and brutal. Many of the men who had fallen had hold of their swords but had not had time to draw them fully from their scabbards before being slain. "They didn't stand a chance, poor fellows, but they will be avenged and the Princess rescued!" said the captain looking about his fallen men, "Now, we must not wait, every minute standing here widens the gap between us and the enemy! Come, let us ride north, the way they ran!" and with that, the captain dug his heals into his horse's sides and it reared up on its hind legs and pushed off in speed through the northernly passage the enemy had created. One by one, the men in the group again followed suit. Soon, they were all travelling at full pace along the passage carved through the woods.

The wood was thickly overgrown, but the machine of the enemy had mowed through it, sending wood from trees splintering to the floor as if they weren't even there! No one knew how they would battle against such a machine, but they knew they must try, they must give it their all; the Princess had to be rescued.

The men had been riding for an hour, and the horses had long since become an uncomfortable means of transport, when Bill Bracket's horse whinnied, broke pace and staggered back with front legs kicking and bucking up and down. The men all returned to his side and calmed his horse. "Bloody snakes", said Bill, "I think one bit my horse around that last bend!" "Steady! She will be fine, only Ankl snakes live here, they aren't poisonous, just give a nasty bite!" said the captain. Kedrick jumped down off his horse and approached the agitated animal, his movements surprisingly gentle. The horse's breath plumed into the dusty air, its nostrils flaring wide, and a wave of radiating heat his him as he knelt beside its foreleg. He ran a cautious, calloused hand down the taut muscle, feeling the frantic thrum of blood beneath the slick, steaming hide. The air around the horse seemed to vibrate with its distress. His nimble fingers traced the leg, sifting through the coarse, sweat-matted hair. Then he found it, two small, pinprick punctures, still weeping a bead of blood, amidst the dust and grime. No swelling, no discolouration, just the faint, almost imperceptible sting of a recent wound. A sigh of relief, audible even over the horse's snorts, escaped Kedrick's lips. "Aye, Captain," he called out, rising slowly, "Just a bite. A small one. The poor beast just got a fright." He patted the horse's neck, a reassuring gesture, and the great animal, though still wary, began to settle, its breath gradually evening out.

Bill Bracket was the first to break from the fold of heroic rescuers by saying, "This is hopeless. They will be miles away by now, we will never catch them now!" The men all barked triumphantly that they would rescue the Princess and chastised Bill for his lack of faith, but secretly, they had all started to think the same thoughts. The enemy had over an hour's head start on them and showed no signs of letting up on that lead. This defeatism irked the captain, and the men all saw the fierceness of his eyes as he took in Bill's words. They expected a chastisement to follow, but instead the captain simply fell silent, deep in thought for a moment and then finally said, "We must push on till dusk and then make camp before the time of long shadows passes altogether. The creatures are taking the Princess back to their own city, and that is where we are going, if we travel at the time of scorch tomorrow, we should make up some time and be on top of them by ......" he stopped part way through a sentence and stared at Kedrick, "............that medallion you are wearing, where did you get it, come here, let me see it!", he said. Kedrick stepped forward, "I err...., I err was given it by my father, it has been in our family for years passed down from father to son." Kedrick answered, whilst holding out the smooth, intricately detailed medallion for the captain to admire the delicate imagery. "Do you know the meaning of the writing around the edge?" enquired the captain. "No, sir! But my grandfather always said it was very important." The captain fell silent again and then startled Bill Bracket we he spoke, "Young Kedrick will be coming with me to seek audience with the Queen; you carry on till the time of long shadows, then make camp, and we will catch up as soon as we can." The men didn't argue with the captain and wished them both a safe return. Turning back to Kedrick, the captain instructed, "Come on, boy, we have miles to travel before the time of long shadows! Get on your horse and keep up!"

The captain gave the impression that he knew exactly what had to be done in any given situation, and he would certainly not entertain any doubt about his actions. "What is so special about my medallion, Sir?" enquired Kedrick. "No time for questions now, young man, we must make good time in our journey; there is not a moment to lose! You will get your answers when you gain an audience with the queen!" said the captain. And with that, both men turned tail and headed off back in the direction they had come from faster than before, as the captain and Kedrick had the two finest horses of the group.

Kedrick could feel his back aching under the strain of all this horse riding; it wasn't something he did often. Not that he wasn't a talented rider, he just generally stayed around the town, it was only rarely that he would venture out on horseback across the fields, and then he would be riding playfully, jumping the hedge rows that separated the fields and scattering the birds that nested there, into the sky, in a mad cluster of feathers and angry twittering. But riding with the captain was an entirely different experience. Kedrick had to constantly concentrate on the path ahead for unknown obstacles, and that kind of concentration becomes tiring very quickly, not to mention the physical strain of guiding his horse at speed. At home, Kedrick knew every blade of grass, and that knowledge lifted the burden of riding tenfold for him. But out here, all the territory was alien, and he found himself trusting the captain's judgment more and more.

"Not far now," exclaimed the captain. Those lights in the sky over there are coming from the castle towers. We must hurry; the time of shadows is nearly fully on us," said the captain as he looked all around in a worried way. "We must hurry!" he repeated as he dug his heels into his trusted steed and sped off in front of Kedrick, who followed suit, soon being back, neck and neck with the captain.

As the city walls came into sight and the flurry of trumpets sounded, followed by the evident clunking of the giant, solid iron gate being cranked open, which reassured them that their journey was nearly over. For years, Kedrick had heard stories about the glorious city of Targon, about the clean, tidy cobbled streets and beautifully crafted buildings, the most impressive of which, of course, was the palace with its perfectly rectangular stone blocks all cut to such precision you could barely see the joins. No one that Kedrick had ever known had possessed the ability to make such precise brickwork, and as his horse thundered after the captains towards the city gate, Kedrick found himself staring at the astounding quality of workmanship that even the city wall displayed. In fact, it had been rumoured that no one alive possessed the ability to replicate these walls, that no one knew who had crafted them or how.

Once they had passed under the city's giant ironwork gate, they rode with haste the full length of the long main street that led from the gate, stretching on past the marketplace and many houses and shops, right to the centre of the city, where the palace was located, enclosed within its own walls. "Here we are!" shouted the captain to Kedrick as another flurry of trumpets set the palace gate clanking open. The captain dismounted his horse in the courtyard and called for an immediate audience with the Queen. His words fell on deaf ears as the chief of the royal court, who had come to greet their visitors, said, "I am sorry, Captain Blade. The Queen is not available for an audience presently, and you should return to your duties and wait to be summoned!" "Balderdash, I have serious matters to discuss with the Queen that cannot wait; the Princess has been kidnapped, and I require an audience immediately." The captain paused briefly and then pushed past the chief and stated quite abruptly, "We will await audience in the diplomatic chamber". "Follow me, Kedrick", the captain's voice, as rough as a grindstone, cut through the dust-laden air. He didn't wait for an answer, his broad back already receding, a silhouette against the shimmering heat. His heavy boots crunched on the sun-baked earth as he marched with an unyielding stride towards the distant shimmer of the palace's inner sanctum. There they stood, impossibly grand and gleaming even from this distance: two towering, gold-encrusted arch doors, massive and imposing, reflecting the harsh sunlight in blinding flashes. They promised both immense power and unimaginable peril beyond their formidable embrace. The interior decor was as breathtaking as the entrance; once inside the diplomatic chamber, Kedrick was struck by the opulent polished stone and the fragrant scent of beeswax and polished oak, both of which hinted at the rich historical significance of the palace. The grand decor featured six enormous pillars down the centre of the chamber, three on either side of a central aisle that extended from the doors to the throne at the far end. Each of the pillars had been made from marble, which was a very rare commodity these days and very expensive. But that wasn't the end of it; each opulent pillar had coloured pictures carved into it, telling stories from the history of Targon. Or at least that was what Kedrick assumed. On the first pillar was a man standing on a hill (in what Kedrick assumed was a distant land, as none of the scenery looked familiar to him), holding what looked like a strange sword, or perhaps even a walking stick, up against a rock. The next bit couldn't be seen due to damage to the pillar. Squinting a little further down on the pillar, it looked like buildings were being built, buildings that may have been the majestic buildings of the city of Targon. The bits that could be seen did look similar, even though they were only half-built in the image.

"Hurry up, Kedrick!" called the captain. Kedrick joined the captain in front of the Throne. "When the Queen enters, we must both kneel on one knee and bow our heads until she tells us to rise. Do you understand, Kedrick?" "Yes, kneel and bow our heads, I've got it", replied Kedrick.

# The Prophecy

They had already been waiting for a little while when Kedrick turned his head to look at the pillar to his right. The pictures in this story were quite familiar to Kedrick. "They should be too", he thought as he recognised in an instant the village where he had been living and working these past few years, Kevlar. "Hang on", he thought to himself, this pillar must have only just been erected, as the statue in the village square in the picture had only just been placed there last year! Maybe the historians had made a mistake and instead of doing proper research, they just went by a recent painting of the village! The next part of the story had a much better picture of the man with the sword, there was something familiar about him too, but Kedrick just couldn't put his finger on it, he was a good looking fellow with brown hair, cut in the same style as Kedrick's, he had a medallion around his neck, but it was impossible to see what was on the medallion. The next picture showed the man and what seemed to be a platoon of men climbing high mountains.

At that moment, Kedrick felt an elbow nudge him in his side, and he quickly dropped down on one knee beside the captain with his head bowed. The Queen had entered the chamber. She walked in front of the two men and sat upon her throne. "You may both arise! Please do tell me what news you have of my daughter, the Princess. Is it true that she has been kidnapped?"

The Queen was rumoured to be forty-three years old, yet she looked only twenty-three and very beautiful. It must be from leading such a privileged life, Kedrick thought. The women in his village, who were only half as old, looked far older. Yes, a hard life leaves hardened features, he thought.

"I am sorry to report it is true, your majesty. The Princess was kidnapped during an ambush halfway down Robber's Lane. All of my men fought bravely in vain, but in injury, they were overcome. I recruited men from the village of Kevlar and set off to rescue the Princess." Then why are you here and without my daughter, Captain Blade? What are you not telling me?" demanded the Queen. "Whilst locating the kidnappers' tracks, by chance, I noticed something familiar about this young recruit's medallion and thought it would be best to bring him to your majesty for immediate counsel, whilst the recruits continued forward after the Princess," answered Captain Blade.

"What is your name, young man?" asked the Queen. "Kedrick, your majesty," replied Kedrick quite nervously. "Step forward and show me your medallion, if you will please," the Queen requested. Kedrick fumbled in his shirt to find the medallion and promptly handed it to the Queen, who then quietly spoke, under her breath, "It has begun…" It was as if her mouth had betrayed her innermost thoughts, and she then fell very quiet and examined the medallion closely. After some time had passed, the Queen asked Kedrick, "Tell me, young man, where did you get this medallion?"

"My Father gave it to me. It has been in our family for years, passed down from father to son," answered Kedrick. I see. Do you know anything else about the medallion, young man?" "No, your majesty, except that my father told me that it was very important and that it should always be kept safe".

Turning towards the Captain, the Queen commented, "You made the right choice, Captain Blade. It appears the prophecy of Ellowed is coming true." "That is my thought too, your majesty", replied the captain. "Tell me, young man, what is your name?" spoke the Queen. "It is Kedrick, your majesty." "Well, Kedrick, if you look at the pictures on these pillars, does anything seem familiar to you at all?" What trickery is this, thought Kedrick, but he answered dutifully, "Of course, the pictures on this new pillar are of my village, Kevlar, your majesty!" "Kedrick? Why do you think this pillar is new?" asked the Queen. "Well, it is the inclusion of the statue in the Village square, your majesty, your scholars must have made a mistake in preparing this pillar, as the statue was only erected last year!" Both the Queen and the Captain exchanged a surprised glance, and then the Queen continued, "Kedrick that is most interesting, all of these pillars are over one hundred years old and were put in place at the time the palace was built, in fact any attempt to remove or replace them would have the palace collapsing upon our heads." "B...b.b. But," stammered Kedrick in disbelief. "This is no trick and certainly no joke, Kedrick, the pillar you mentioned to your right and the pillar to your left contain pictures drawn by a man called Ellowed who lived when this palace was built. He was a spiritual man, and many said he could see what the future held. Before his death, he drew detailed pictures of a quest that one man would undertake for the good of all Mantle. The drawings are known as the Ellowed Prophecy, and these are those drawings, and the prophecy states that the man, the saviour, will come from that village in the picture that you identified as your village of Kevlar." "What is more, Kedrick, if you look at the pillar to your left, it shows clearly the medallion that the man will wear", said the Queen calmly.

The captain stepped back to allow Kedrick a closer look and as Kedrick looked, he just couldn't believe what his eyes were telling him, the medallion was identical to his, or at least it appeared to be as he couldn't fully see it due to the damage that had occurred to the pillar so the outer edge of the medallion had writing missing from it, but the rest of it was spot on.

He stepped back, speechless. "Kedrick, it would appear that you are that man, and you are destined to go on this quest into the forbidden land to the east." The Queen paused for a while and then continued, "It was no random act that led to my daughter, the Princess, being kidnapped today; it was fate acting upon our lives to bring us together. Captain Blade, we must not be hasty in our next steps; we will meet again in the morning to decide what our next action should be," said the Queen. "Servants, please show our guest Kedrick to the Ambassador's suite and provide him with new attire and a good meal." "We will speak more in the morning. Now I must retire to think more about today's happenings. Good day to you both."

Both the captain and Kedrick bowed as the Queen left the chamber. "There is some mistake, Captain Blade. I am no hero, no saviour. I am a miller's apprentice, that is all!" said Kedrick in mild panic, feeling he was going insane. "I know this all must be very hard to take in, Kedrick, but you yourself told me that your father had told you the medallion was very important, you do come from that village in the picture, and the man with the medallion in the picture bears an uncanny resemblance to you!" replied the captain. "Ye...ss. I, I know, b, b, but", said Kedrick. "Sometimes in life, the road we are on is unclear to us until we have travelled halfway along, a lot of choices are made for us, and all we can do is decide whether to act bravely and do our best or to run and hide away. My advice to you is to do your best, you don't have to be a hero or a saviour, just be Kedrick." The captain's words calmed Kedrick's mind, and he felt a lot easier, knowing that all the captain expected from him was to be himself. "Thank you, captain," said Kedrick. "I will see you in the morning. Go and relax and get some sleep if you can."

As the captain left the chamber, the servants ushered Kedrick through a door, along a hall, and then up what seemed to be a million steps to the top of a tower. "This is the Ambassador Suite, Sir. You will find a change of clothing in the wardrobes in the next room, and food has been ordered for you from the royal kitchen and should arrive shortly. If you find you need anything, please ring the bell rope by the door, and I will come to your assistance", said the Servant. "Is there anything else, sir?" "No, thank you", answered Kedrick. "Very well, Sir. Good day, Sir", the servant said whilst walking backwards out the door. "Good day", Kedrick said to the servant's shadow.

"What dream am I in?" thought Kedrick. "I am awake, aren't I?" he asked himself, pinching his arm hard. "OWW! Yes, I guess that answers that question; I am not dreaming."

The room was laid out magnificently to impress foreign ambassadors with the skills and crafts of the people of Targon; every item in the room was top quality, and the settee looked so comfortable that Kedrick dared not sit down on it for fear of never wanting to get up again. The balcony captured his attention, and he strolled forward to take in the view. It was breathtaking.

In the distance, Kedrick could see his home village of Kevlar, along with fishing boats on the sea. The wind carried a faint scent of salt and seaweed, which made him feel a twinge of homesickness. Kedrick had never seen such a view before. They brought a meal for Kedrick, and he sat on a balcony chair and ate and stared out to the horizon, rediscovering the world in which he lived from an entirely new angle.

That night, Kedrick slept soundly, better than he ever had before. "What a privilege it is to be able to sleep on a bed so fine and comfortable", he thought to himself as he awoke the next day to the noise of a bird chirping on the balcony rail. Unbeknownst to Kedrick, he was being treated to an audience with the rarest of rare birds, the Peligonhedrial. A creature of exquisite refinement, perched delicately on the wrought-iron railing of his balcony. Its plumage, a shimmering tapestry of iridescent blues and greens, caught in the sunlight, each feather seeming to hold a fragment of the morning sky. Its neck, long and gracefully curved, gave it an almost regal bearing, while its bright, intelligent eyes, like polished obsidian, keenly observed the hero within Kedrick. It was rumoured that Peligonhedrial's had faded out of existence and had become creatures of legend, but in truth, the entire colony of Peligonhedrial's had simply, like the wizard had had enough of the ridiculous behaviour of the people, and for these highly strung birds, wearing croaking hats on their heads had been the final straw. Therefore, following a vote by the elders, the entire colony had moved further north, closer to the mountains, near the house of Asthal.

But now the wisest of these birds had been chosen by the elders to travel to Targon to meet with Kedrick at this time, because their own prophecy demanded that they thank Kedrick the Valiant for saving their race.

With a sudden, almost imperceptible tremor, the Peligonhedrial began to sing. It was a cascade of intricate trills and warbles, a language woven from the very air, imbued with a passion and reverence that transcended mere sound. The notes soared and dipped, echoing the bird's profound admiration, extolling our unwitting hero's courage, his unwavering spirit, and the quiet nobility of his heart. Though Kedrick only heard a beautiful, alien melody, unaware of the profound praise being lavished upon him, the bird continued his ode, its chest swelling with the depth of its unspoken devotion, a truly elegant spectacle. Then, after extolling Kedrick's virtues openly to him and not realising for one second that Kedrick could not understand a single word the beautifully strange-looking bird on the balcony was saying, he left, feeling quite content that he had performed his role most adequately. As Kedrick arose fully from his slumber, he found an exceptional, luxurious breakfast had been left for him on the bedside table. Everything bar a slice or two of loaf he thought as he had a drink of Imperial Tae and eyed up the finely sliced and marinated Hog meat, which had been cooked till crispy. Suddenly, there was a knock at the door, and Kedrick summoned in a palace servant, "You may enter!".

"The Queen would like to meet with you in chambers after your breakfast, and here are your new clothes, at the Queen's request." And with that, the servant stepped forward into the room fully and placed a splendid-looking set of clothes over a chair. "Thank you, Sir!" the servant said as he bowed forward and retreated out of the room. The suit of clothes reminded Kedrick of the young man in the historical pictures he had been shown yesterday; they echoed Knightlines, and as he put them on, a warmth, unlike any he'd ever known, bloomed in Kedrick's chest as the unfamiliar fabric settled against his skin. These weren't the roughspun tunics he was used to; this was the touch of the Queen's own weavers, a whisper of silk and the solid reassurance of fine wool. Each seam, each stitch, spoke of purpose and strength. The deep sapphire blue of the tunic seemed to deepen the colour of his eyes, and the silver embroidery, subtly gleaming, hinted at the gleam of a knight's polished armour. He ran a hand over the sleeve, feeling the rich texture, and a quiet sense of awe unfurled within him. It wasn't just clothing; it was a transformation. With every breath, he felt a little taller, a little broader. The weight of the garments, though light, carried the profound weight of expectation, not a burden, but a promise. He felt newfound dignity, a sense of belonging to something greater than himself. Could this be how real knights felt? He wondered. A flicker of courage, tentative at first, then bolder, ignited his spirit. He imagined himself on the battlefield, not as humble Kedrick, but as a figure of valour, clad in these very colours. The clothes were a shield, yes, but more than that, they were an affirmation. They didn't just cover him; they revealed a potential he hadn't dared to dream of, making him feel, for the first time, truly special, truly worthy. He had never expected such a turn of events, never expected that he would be wearing such fine clothes. Even the elders of his village didn't have clothes of such finery. In fact, their clothes were quite old and ragged, even their best suits, kept for the arrival of dignitaries, were all old and mothballed looking. Kedrick had been having a tough time assessing the new information that he was special, but now he felt imbued with the quiet strength and budding courage of a knight.

He rushed through his breakfast and then searched for the royal chambers. After many wrong turns, he finally found his way. Kedrick knocked on the door. "Enter", spoke the Queen, "AH, Good morning, Kedrick, come in front of me!"

"Yes, your majesty", Kedrick replied. "Kneel" – Kedrick wondered why the Queen wanted him to kneel in front of her having little knowledge of royal matters, but he knew one thing for sure, if the Queen says kneel, you kneel – so he did. The Queen then tapped him on either shoulder with a sword garnished with colourful gems. "Arise, Sir Kedrick the Valiant!" said the Queen. Kedrick stood up, astonished that he had been knighted by the Queen. "Sir Kedrick, after we spoke yesterday, I

summoned my historians to investigate your lineage, it is written in the royal records that Elwood is your ancestor, your family has in secret been guarding that medallion over the centuries and passing it down from generation to generation in order for it to be given to you in readiness for your quest." "You are to be our saviour, Kedrick – it is written in the ancient prophecy that this day would come and that you would succeed in your quest, but it is also written that you will need help!" As the Queen spoke, she waved her hand in the direction of the captain, who was standing behind Kedrick, "Captain Blade will accompany you on your quest; you will also need the help of a powerful Sorcerer. You must travel to seek the assistance of Asthal the Great; he will guide you from there."
Both Kedrick and Captain Blade knew not what to say and simply nodded in agreement with the Queen. "This will aid you in battle, Sir Kedrick", said the Queen, handing a sword to Kedrick. As the Queen extended her hand, Kedrick's gaze fell upon the sword, and his breath hitched. It was unlike any blade he had ever seen. Not the crude iron of a farmer's tool, nor the functional steel of a guard's weapon. This was a sliver of solidified moonlight, or perhaps a captured whisper of the dawn. Its surface, a muted silver, seemed to drink the light of the chamber, never glinting harshly, yet hinting at an inner luminescence. "It is one of the original blades of Targon, perhaps the last one", the Queen continued. He reached out, his fingers trembling,

and felt its impossible lightness. It settled in his palm as if it were a feather, yet a quiet hum vibrated through its hilt, speaking of unbreakable strength, far surpassing any steel. It was a contradiction, a paradox of perfection. But, it was more than just its material form that captivated him. The moment his hand closed around the grip, a startling sensation flowed through him. It wasn't just the cold metal, but a sudden, vivid clarity, a whisper of understanding that settled deep within his bones. He felt a sudden, profound knowing of the blade, as if it had always been an extension of his own arm. His fingers instinctively adjusted, his wrist subtly angled, and he felt a phantom dance of parries and thrusts, a graceful, lethal ballet unfolding in his mind's eye. It was as if the sword itself was guiding his very thoughts, offering ancient lessons in swordmanship, a silent tutor awakening a dormant skill he never knew he possessed. This was not merely a weapon; it was a partner, a mentor, a piece of Targon's legacy now intertwined with his own destiny.

The Queen smiled, seeing how Kedrick was taken with the blade, truly seeing the knight within him surface fully. "I wish you both luck in your quest and ask that you hasten on your way to Asthal". "Thank you, your majesty," both men said together as the Queen royally bowed her head, and both men turned and left the room.

"I have so many questions, Captain Blade! Nothing makes sense anymore!" said Kedrick. "Nonsense, Sir

Kedrick, nothing has changed, we have a mission to save the Princess, and we will do it! If along the way we must seek counsel from Asthal the wizard, then we shall do so; now let us get our horses and ride", ordered the captain.

# The Quest Begins

"We have a long ride. Asthal lives on the far edge of the Xendar Forest; it will take us all of two days riding to reach him, so tonight we will be making camp in the Forest of Xendar."

Whilst Kedrick and the Captain manoeuvred through the Forest of Xendar, the Princess's rescue party rode on hard in the hope the captain would soon return to them.

Bill Bracket was enjoying the role of commanding officer after being out of service for so many long years; he felt that he had purpose again. He knew he had a job to do, and he would do it well. He knew their enemy was strong and fast, from the brutal attack the captain had described. Bill also knew that his men were not trained soldiers. Still, a mixed bunch of hot-headed farmers and labourers, even he was no longer a soldier, sure, he had the training and the experience, but that was a long time ago, and he knew only too well his skill at arms had become rusty, at best. With this in mind, he figured a surprise night raid to free the Princess, minimising contact with the enemy, followed by a hasty retreat, would be the way to go. They would have to watch their enemy's movements as soon as they catch up; study what they do each night, where they keep the

Princess, and how often they change guard. Then they would have to wait for an opportunity to present itself before striking. "The men need to know what to do, or we will stand no chance of pulling this off! Before we make camp tonight, I will run some drills with the men", he thought, 'You cannot be too prepared.'

"Another couple of hours till we stop for the night", said the captain "We need to pick up the pace if we are going to make camp before the hour of long shadows is upon us!" Kedrick nodded to the captain. The first few hoofs into Xendar Forest had been deceptively familiar. The air carried the scent of damp earth and pine needles that calmed the soul. A gentle breeze rustled the leaves overhead, creating a soft, vibrant whisper. Patches of sunlight dappled the forest floor, illuminating vibrant green moss and the occasional shy wildflower through the gaps in the branches. On the surface, it was simply a forest like countless others. But as Kedrick rode deeper, the rhythmic thud of his horse's hooves became the only steady sound, and an insidious shift began. The canopy, initially a welcoming embrace and escape from the torturous sun's rays, thickened, weaving together into an impenetrable ceiling. The sunlight, once playful, became a distant memory, replaced by a perpetual twilight. The air grew heavy, still and strangely cold, carrying a faint metallic tang, like old blood on damp stone. The chirping of birds, which had accompanied their entry, dwindled, replaced by an unnerving silence broken only by the snorts and soft breathing of the horses. The trees themselves seemed to lean in, their ancient, gnarled branches twisting like arthritic fingers, casting elongated, shifting shadows that danced with an unseen rhythm in a breeze that could not be felt. Every rustle of leaves, every snap of a twig, no longer felt like the benign movements of wildlife, but rather a deliberate stir, a shifting of unseen mass. Kedrick felt the prickle of unseen eyes upon him, a chilling awareness of being observed from the impenetrable depths between the trunks, a sensation that raised the hairs on the back of his neck. The forest breathed, but it was a cold, slow breath, a watchful, patient presence that seeped into his very bones, leaving him with an undeniable, unsettling certainty: they were not alone, and this was not any forest. It was a place that felt alive, and it was watching.

For an hour, Kedrick hadn't seen as much as a squirrel or a Mudlark, which are very common in all other forests. So, the suggestion that they travel faster suited Kedrick, the less time in this forest the better he thought and pushed his horse onwards harder than before, by digging his heal into her flanks and at the same time whispering in her ear, "Come on my beauty, we need to go faster, you can do it!" And she did, matching that of the captains. Mile after mile, they pushed on until at last the dense, oppressive gloom of Xendar Forest finally began to thin. Kedrick, hunched in his saddle, felt his shoulders ease as the gnarled branches above started to give way to wider gaps of sky.

Then, with a final push through a curtain of intertwined saplings, they broke through. A gasp of pure, unadulterated relief escaped him, though he quickly suppressed it. Before them lay a small, natural clearing, a gentle bowl scooped out of the forest's dark heart. The air here was different, fresher, lighter, free from the stagnant chill of the deeper woods. And then, a sound he hadn't realised he'd missed: the tentative, sweet chirp of a robin, followed by another, and another, until a symphony of evening birdsong began to weave through the air. The clearing itself was unassuming, a patch of worn grass encircled by the watchful, yet now less menacing, trees. A faint scent of wildflowers, crushed underfoot by deer perhaps, mingled with the damp earth. In the centre, the ground was slightly higher, offering a natural dry spot for the fire.

"Here," Captain Blade's voice, though low, cut through the quiet, carrying a note of satisfaction. He dismounted with practised ease, his movements fluid even after the tense ride. "We'll make camp for the night. You take the sleep, Kedrick. I'll take first watch." The words were a balm, a promise of respite. Kedrick slid off his horse; his legs were stiff, and his back ached, but with a profound sense of weariness and gratitude washing over him, the aches didn't bother him. Within minutes, the simple ritual of setting up camp began. The horses were tethered to a low-hanging branch, munching contentedly. Captain Blade, with an efficiency born of countless nights spent under the stars, quickly gathered dry twigs and fallen branches. Soon, a small campfire sputtered to life, its tentative orange glow pushing back the encroaching shadows. The crackle and hiss of the flames further settled Kedrick's mind, and the warmth radiating outwards became the true heart of their sanctuary, a beacon against the lingering unease of the surrounding forest. The night might be cold, but for now, in this small, illuminated circle, they were safe. "I will take the first watch. You can get some sleep now. I will wake you when it is your turn." "Sounds good to me", said Kedrick, who was, in all fairness, more tired than the captain anyway. Seconds later, Kedrick was snoring his head off; he wasn't used to all this riding, and it had tired him out.

In his dreams, whilst Captain Blade stood watch, Kedrick saw a mighty battle against the creatures they had chased. He was standing in the middle of an opening in a forest, and he wielded a gold-hilted sword, slaying creature after creature in an open display of expert swordsmanship. Then Kedrick's dream altered, and the forest started to sink away from his feet. Hang on, the forest wasn't sinking, he thought to himself in the dream; he was floating, rising up alongside the tallest trees in the forest. Whilst most would have loved the sensation of flight, it disturbed Kedrick greatly as he didn't like heights, not one bit. But his dream wouldn't listen to him, and his cries of concern went unnoticed as he floated higher, now he was above the treetops and floating forward, quicker and quicker towards the mountains, past the river of confusion. Kedrick looked down on the trees, he was moving so fast now all he could see was a streaking blur of Green, a glint of blue as he crossed the river and then a blur of green again, a tapestry unfolding at an impossible speed. But he was still moving faster and faster. He felt the air, thin and exhilarating, pressing against his face, a tangible force pushing back against his very bones. It grew stronger, a relentless, roaring current that threatened to tear the breath from his lungs and reshape his features. The sheer onslaught of imagery was staggering. Forests rushed beneath him like fuzzy green carpets, rivers a glimmering blue ribbon, mountains rising and falling in dizzying waves. Details flashed and vanished too quickly to register: a distant tower, a herd of deer scattering, the intricate pattern of fields. His eyes, wide with wonder and exhilaration, tried desperately to grasp it all, to catalogue the impossible beauty and speed, but it was too much. The world was a kaleidoscope of fleeting colours and shapes, a dizzying, overwhelming spectacle. Finally, with a soft exhale, he didn't realise he's been holding, Kedrick squeezed his eyes shut. The force of the wind, now unimpeded, screamed past his ears, a powerful, abstract roar. The vibrant, chaotic flood of visuals was replaced by the velvet blackness of his eyelids, a necessary retreat from sensory overload. Then, suddenly, he felt his body jerk to stillness. Quite stunned, he opened his eyes again to find himself standing motionless on top of a mountain, the biting wind whipping strands of hair across his face. The dream's exhilarating speed had vanished, replaced by the stark, silent majesty of a mountaintop.

Before him, the peak plunged into a dizzying abyss, but his gaze was fixed, not on the vastness below, but on something directly ahead: a rock formation unlike any other he had witnessed. It wasn't merely a pile of boulders; it was a sculpture wrought by aeons, a colossal, twisted embrace of stone that seemed to writhe from the earth itself. And nestled within its shadowed heart was an opening, a cave entrance that was more than just a void. It was a mouth, vast and irregular, framed by jagged teeth of ancient rock. |The air around it felt different, colder, yet strangely alive, carrying a faint earthy scent mixed with something else, something ancient and profound. No light penetrated its depths, only an absolute inky blackness that seemed to absorb the very concept of illumination. Yet, despite the darkness, it wasn't foreboding in the usual sense. Instead, it hummed with a palpable mystery, a deep, resonant silence that spoke of untold secrets. It felt less like a hole in the mountain and more like a threshold, an invitation to a hidden world, a world that beckoned to Kedrick. Instilling in him a desperate ache to enter the cave, to find the answers withheld from him. It wasn't just a cave, it was a call, a powerful, undeniable summons to step into the unknown and discover whatever ancient truth lay waiting within its shadowy embrace. Kedrick strained to see more of the cave opening, and then he heard a voice. "Kedrick, you must travel here, you must enter this cave, you are the chosen one!"

Then the voice became stern and shouted, "Now grab your sword, get on your feet, you are under attack!" Kedrick jumped awake and instinctively followed orders, he grabbed his sword and held it ready to strike as a creature lunged at him trying to land a spear through his chest, he shifted to the right and swung his right arm bringing the sword squarely down on the creatures neck landing a deafly blow that put his foe to the ground, but there was no time to think about his victorious fight, as another creature was flanking to his right. In an instant, he was deflecting the parry of a creature's sword; he spun around and cut the sword out of the creature's hands before bringing his sword down on the creature.

Now Kedrick saw more creatures, emerging from the inky blackness beyond the fire's reach were five shapes, hunched and fast, moving with an unnerving, almost animalistic grace. They weren't men, not as Kedrick knew them. These were … things. Their forms were obscured by a dense, matted covering of what looked like long, shaggy hair, so thick it seemed to absorb the meagre light of the fire, making them appear as shadowy, indistinct masses. There was no clear outline of face or limb, only an impression of heavy brows, deep-set eyes, and an unsettling, broad, powerful build beneath the fur. The captain was fighting two of them, and the other three were closing in on Kedrick's left and right flanks. He held his sword in front of him, his left hand undoing the scabbard whilst watching the creatures closing in by their reflection on his sword. Gripping the sword tightly in his right hand, he felt a sudden surge of spirit soar through his veins. His heart pumped fast, and he couldn't think. He just acted, spinning around, throwing his scabbard at the creatures to his left, whilst side-stepping to the right, spinning around again and then bringing his sword down again upon his enemy, killing him with a single blow. The creatures to the left had recovered from the scabbard throw, and both lurched dangerously at him. He penetrated one, putting his sword through the creature's chest, but was not quick enough to defend against the second, and he fell backwards to the ground, trying to avoid the sword. Just as he thought he was done for, that all hope had left, the creature fell to his knees, looking squarely into the eyes of Kedrick before completing his final motion to the ground. Left in his wake was the captain and a sword dripping with blood.

The captain helped Kedrick to his feet whilst keeping an eye on the periphery. They took stock of their surroundings, readying themselves for further battle, but nothing moved; all was still. They stood quietly, waiting for the next attack. Fifteen agonising minutes crawled by, each one a stretched-out moment of coiled tension. Kedrick, still trembling slightly, kept his sword raised, his eyes darting into the impenetrable darkness beyond the campfire's flickering reach. Every rustle of leaves, every distant snap of a twig, sent a jolt of ice through him, bracing him for another attack by the monstrous, shaggy figures.

However, the silence, a heavy, watchful silence, was the only enemy now. Captain Blade, a statue of readiness beside him, finally lowered his blade with a soft chink as it tapped and then rested on the stony ground at his feet. His posture, which had been rigid with expectation, visibly softened. "No more," he stated, his voice a low rumble, devoid of the earlier urgency. "If there were others, they'd have moved on us by now. They hit hard and fast, or they don't hit at all." A profound, almost dizzying wave of exhaustion washed over Kedrick as he accepted the knowledgeable words of the captain. He hadn't realised how tightly strung every muscle had been, or how shallow his breathing was. He let his own sword fall to his side, the weight of it suddenly immense. The air. Which had tasted of iron and fear, now carried the comforting scent of woodsmoke once more.

The captain turned, his movements now slow and deliberate, a stark contrast to his earlier battle-ready stance. He walked to the struggling campfire, its embers now a dim, pulsing heart in the gloom. With a quiet sigh, he arranged a few more small branches, coaxing a fresh flicker of warmth. He then settled down, not with a collapse, but with the controlled descent of a man utterly spent yet still disciplined. "It's my turn to sleep, your turn for watch duty, wake me if anything occurs!"

Kedrick realised that the danger had passed and slowly eased up his stance and moved to the fireside, sat on a log, and started watching the flames of the fire dancing about. "If I were home, now I could have a hot cup of Caffa, put my feet up, and drift off to sleep by the fire!" he said silently to himself. Caffa was much like hot chocolate, but with a slight corny taste to it. But Kedrick wasn't at home, and dreaming about being home only made him feel worse. "Never mind", he told himself, "At least tomorrow we will arrive at Asthal's house, perhaps he has some Caffa!"

The night dragged on, and on numerous occasions, Kedrick felt his head fall out of the fine balance held upon his hand and suddenly jumped awake, having just nodded off! "Oh well, at least the horses are doing the work today!" a very tired Kedrick thought.

Thankfully, the rest of the night passed without incident, apart from an annoying Gurkowl that cried out every now and then all through the night. Gurkowls are large, smelly, nocturnal birds that exist purely due to another magic spell that went wrong!

Again, Asthal's apprentice was to blame. Who had been trying to conjure up a spell to cook a turkey in record time, because he had forgotten to put his masters Christmas turkey on to cook when he should have, so he stood in the kitchen of the wizard's house, ringing out combinations of magical spells in a vain attempt to get the turkey to cook instantly!

The kitchen was a chaotic symphony of scents and textures. A thick, warm current hummed with an underlying tone of dust and old parchment, mingled with the sharp bite of herbs; thyme, rosemary, and something else, metallic and faintly sweet, like crushed stars. Shelves, bowing under the weight of countless jars and stoppered bottles, lined every wall. Some held glistening, preserved newt eyes, others glowing powders that shimmered faintly, and many more were filled with dried, rusting bundles of plants, their leaves brittle to the touch.

On the long, scarred worktable, by which Grundlenut now stood in a deepening puddle of despair, lay the raw, unadorned Christmas turkey. Its skin was pallid, slightly greasy white, and dotted with the ghosts of plucked feathers. A faint chill radiated from the bird, a raw, fleshy scent that cut through the kitchen's usual aromas. A film of sweat was starting to bead on Grundlenut's brow, partly from the heat of his frantic attempts, partly from his sheer panic. Around him, the kitchen offered a cacophony of small, insistent sounds. The slow drip of a leaky tap into a stone sink, the soft creak of a broom leaning against a wall, the almost inaudible rustle of something scuttling behind a stack of grimoires. Light, filtering through a small, grimy window, cast skewed, dancing shadows from a collection of bronze cauldrons and glass alembics hanging from the ceiling, their surfaces dulled by time and unknown residues. A faint, resinous smell clung to the area near the large, imposing hearth, where a massive, soot-blackened oven gaped silently, its interior cold and unwelcoming. Every surface, from the flagstone floor beneath Grundlenut's trembling boots to the intricate carvings on the wizard's high-backed stool, was coated in a fine, almost magical layer of grime and forgotten dust, a testament to Asthal's singular focus on arcana over cleanliness.

The despairing apprentice had already tried quite a few combinations of spells, to little or no effect. "Turkey on the baking tray, cook your fastest ever!" which failed as all that happened was that the turkey magically transported to the oven, and so did a few extra logs, intended to make the oven hotter than its usual cooking temperature! The apprentice wanted the turkey cooked, not just burnt, so he countered the spell and removed the bird from the oven. Standing over the raw, uncooked bird sitting on the table, he started to utter a new, undisciplined incantation. His concoction of words fell sharply, far from the teachings of his master, who, if he were watching him, would have reminded him about the importance of specifics in spell casting! "Let this bird be alive... with flavour... Let me smell its scent... let it be ready, now!" Suddenly, there was a big flash of light and a bang, and the apprentice was knocked backwards, onto the floor by the power his spell had unleashed!

By the time he came to his senses and got up, the bird was gone, and the air was filled with a sharp, acrid scent, mixed with the lingering smell of scorched earth and a faint, metallic tang, which was quickly fading. He didn't realise what he had done, but suddenly two miles away in Xendar forest, a new species of bird simply blinked into being, the Gurkey!

The apprentice tried many times to counter his spell, but because he did not for one moment realise that he had actually created a new life form, his attempts were pointless, and he was unable to get his counter spell to work.

Eventually, he told Asthal that a fox had stolen the bird after it had been cooked and was waiting to be brought to the table. At that point, the wise old wizard simply muttered something incoherently, and a large, cooked turkey appeared on his table, and that was that.

But life for the Gurkey was tough; it had a very strong scent that, quite frankly, caused great discomfort to any creature nearby. It frankly just stank awfully, and it was only the local skunks that seemed not to mind. Had anyone been brave enough to contend with the smell and catch and cook the bird, the reward would have been a tasty meal, as it did have a lovely flavour. But whenever anyone caught a whiff of the terrible scent, they just turned and ran away. And on went the solitary life of the Gurkey for several seasons, living a lonely, isolated life away from all the forest creatures bar the skunks. Forced to live off tree bark, leaves and plants that were rooted solidly in the ground and unable to run away. That was the Gurkey's life, at least until one day, when the Gurkey came across a large owl that had, she explained, not long since flown into a tree after smelling something awful that screwed up her senses, causing her to lose track of her flying. It appeared that on the whole, she was ok but couldn't smell anything at all! They immediately became friends, and thankfully for the Gurkey, the Owl never realised that the smell that caused her to crash into a tree was actually the evil scent of the Gurkey. Over time, they grew close and mated, and their offspring became the new species of bird known as the Gurkowl. People had thought the birds had moved in from another land far away and hoped that the smelly things would move back there one day soon!

As the first rays of sunlight touched Captain Blade's face, he woke and sprang up from his slumbering position with such get-up-and-go that Kedrick, who was half nodding off to sleep, fell back in shock! "Come on, Sir Kedrick, let us cook up some breakfast, and then we will continue our journey!" said the captain in a strong, commanding tone. His young accomplice collected some more wood, as he had used the previous day's stock of wood throughout the night, keeping the fire going.

The captain then rustled through his bags and found some loaf and a couple of thick rashers of hog's meat. The smell of the Hog's meat cooking almost proved too much for Kedrick; his stomach had been rumbling for half of the night, and he just wanted to grab the food off the stick the captain was using to hold it above the fire and eat it there and then. He had realised that when you stay awake all night, you actually get very hungry. But Kedrick controlled himself and waited patiently for the captain to finish preparing breakfast.

Once breakfast was ready, however, Kedrick tucked into his portion with the ferocity of a wild animal. It was gone in seconds, but it had tasted nice. Now it was time to break camp and continue their journey. "Should we just leave their bodies there?" Kedrick asked the captain.

"They wouldn't bury ours, and I sure as heck won't bury theirs, and we don't have the time to waste; we must get moving!" answered the captain.

The men had caught up with the enemy yesterday and had followed them to their base. Now they were sitting just out of sight, at the edge of the mountains of Sunoon. The wind, crisp and thin, whipped at the cloaks of the ragtag rescue party. Below them, nestled against the foothills, lay the enemy garrison.

The air here was sharp with the scent of pine and cold stone, and a faint, acrid smell of woodsmoke drifted up from the encampment.

Bill Bracket, his face grim and set, knelt behind a sparse cluster of wind-stunted evergreens, a temporary commander with the weight of a princess on his shoulders. He scanned the garrison through a makeshift spyglass, his eyes tracing the outlines of watchtowers and the occasional glint of a sentry's armour. The setting sun, a bruised orange smear above the distant horizon, cast long, distorted shadows over the landscape, painting the mountainsides in hues of deep purple and charcoal. The sounds carried deceptively far in the thin mountain air: the distant, rhythmic clang of a hammer from within the garrison walls, the lowing of tethered beasts, and the occasional, muffled shout of a guard. Every one of these sounds seemed amplified, a constant reminder of the danger that lay just within reach.

The ground beneath them was unforgiving, a mix of loose shale and stubborn rock that offered little comfort or cover. The party huddled close, a tight knot of hushed breaths and nervous anticipation. Their faces, etched with fatigue and apprehension, reflected the shared tension. Each minute stretched, taut and silent, as they waited under Bill's command for the last vestiges of daylight to fade, for the vast, encompassing blanket of night to descend and offer them the cover they desperately needed. The chill deepened with the encroaching darkness, a cold that seeped into the bones and mingled with the cold grip of anxiety. They were poised on the precipice, their mission hanging on the fragile thread of stealth and the desperate hope of a successful snatch-and-grab under the moonless sky.

"What do we do now, Bill? Err, Sir, I mean", said one of the men. "We will wait here till nightfall and plan our attack; we will attack once it goes dark!" he answered. Bill had really wanted to wait for the captain to join them, but there was no sign that would happen anytime soon, and he worried for the safety of the princess. If they were to move her to a more secure location, they might lose this opportunity. No, he simply couldn't lose this opportunity; they would strike tonight, in the darkness. He just prayed the captain would turn up before.

# Asthal's Counsel

The air, which had been thick with the damp, earthy scent of the forest, now grew fragrant with the sweet perfume of unseen blossoms. After a long, wearying ride, Captain Blade and Kedrick emerged from the treeline into a small sun-dappled clearing.

There, nestled amongst ancient oaks draped in moss, stood Asthal's home. It was not a tower, nor a looming fortress of stone. Instead, it was a house of profound, enchanting grace, as if it had been lovingly coaxed from the very heart of the forest itself. Its walls were not built of brick, but of smooth honey-coloured wood, intricately carved with swirling patterns of vines and leaves that seemed to still be growing, alive with a quiet magic. Windows, framed in dark, polished oak, were not uniform squares, but a charming patchwork of different sizes and shapes, each pane catching the last golden light of the day and glinting like a jewel. A garden, wild and untamed yet impossibly beautiful, spilt from the base of the house. Fat, velvety roses of impossible blues and silvers climbed the walls, their petals heavy with the evening dew. Vines of ivy, interwoven with tiny, star-like flowers that pulsed with a faint, silvery light, clung to the eaves. The scent of these strange, luminous flowers mingled with the earthy sweetness of the night-blooming jasmine hung in the air like a benevolent mist. The roof, thatched with layers of deep green moss and vibrant ferns, looked like a hillock of enchanted velvet. Smoke, thin and fragrant with the scent of herbs and ancient wood, curled from a stone chimney, a gentle ribbon of welcome against the deepening twilight. The whole house didn't feel like a structure so much as a living, breathing part of the forest, a place of peace and old magic that seemed to sigh with a deep and ancient contentment.

Their presence was immediately felt, even before they reached the front door. As if by magic, it opened, and moments later, they were warmly greeted by Asthal. Once inside, the quest for academic knowledge was clear for all to see, with dusty old magic books cluttering every inch of space possible, piled up even against the edges of the walls. "You are hungry, come let us eat!" commanded the wise wizard, leading the duo into a large dining room with a large empty table in the middle. Asthal walked up to the table and then started walking alongside it towards the far end of the table. As he walked, he raised his right arm over the table, gave it a wave, and the table filled up with the most delicious foods known.

Captain Blade took a seat, and Kedrick followed suit, not wanting to be left standing awkwardly! But he felt a burning fire inside him, they had been sent on a mission to seek this sage's audience by the Queen, this matter cannot be left he thought and uttered, "With all respect

Sir, we have been sent by the Queen to gain coun...",
with a wave of the wizard's hand, Kedrick was silenced.
"I know why you are here, and you will gain my counsel
after we have eaten! Now, please enjoy your food!".
With that, he tucked into his starter, which was chicken
soup. After just a spoonful of the soup, it appeared that
Asthal was wearing more of it on his long, white beard
than he had actually eaten. But then his beard moved as
if it had been blown by a gentle breath of wind, and the
soup stains just vanished, dissolving into thin air!
Kedrick couldn't believe his eyes and stared at the
wizard's beard, catching the wizard's eye by doing so.
He frowned at first, wondering if, somehow, he had
misjudged this young man in his midst, who he was
convinced was the "chosen one". He could not stand ill-
mannered people, and there are just far too many of
them in this world, he thought. But then, he realised
what Kedrick had been staring at and his frown turned
to a gentle smile. "Just an old wizard's spell, that's all it
is!" he said, "I love my beard, but can't stand it being
thick with food, so I put a spell on it to keep it clean!"
"Ohh!" replied Kedrick, relieved that he wasn't seeing
things.

The rest of the meal continued without incident, and
as it drew to a close, the wizard ushered the captain and
Kedrick into his study, which was perfectly round,
boasting three great arched windows on one side and
wall-to-wall bookcases on the other, with a door in the
middle. Looking out of them, Kedrick saw the glow of

Targon City in the distance. He started to drift away in thought of his home, but his daydreams were rudely interrupted when he was addressed, "Kedrick, you are indeed destined to go on a quest, but you must start your quest alone; you must venture to the Mountains of Ellowed. You will have to journey the long way around the Great Lake of Misgiving, as there are many garrisons in the foothills of the mountains. You must keep your wits about you as you cross the plains of confusion, for it will be difficult. I will lend you every advantage my magic can afford you."

Asthal turned to the captain, "For now, your destiny lies upon a different path! Your men have followed the creatures to their garrison base in the foothills of the Mountains of Sunoon! They have seen the Princess and are waiting until dark before they attack! You must rejoin your men and lead them!" "But!" the captain began. It could be seen that the sun was low in the sky already! It was plainly obvious to all what was troubling the captain. He continued, "Surely, I will not reach them in time before they attack; it will be nightfall before I get there." "Don't worry, Captain Blade, I took it upon myself to inform your men that you will soon arrive and to wait for you before they attack!" "But... how did you?" asked the captain. "I sent an echo of myself carrying the message, it will seek out the man you left in charge and deliver the message as clearly as if I were standing right in front of him and then melt away into thin air. You must ride, captain, your men await your arrival, but first, I need to have a word with you in private", spoke the wizard as he guided the captain out of the study, whilst talking in a low, inaudible voice.

Moments later, the wizard reappeared and then spent the next two hours briefing Kedrick on what he was to do and what he had to beware of. It seemed the biggest danger was that of losing his mind when crossing the Plains of Confusion, which would be his biggest test. Once he had faced that challenge, his next was to climb the biggest of the mountains of Ellowed and enter the cave at the top, as he had done in his dream. His dream, it turned out, was provided to him kindly by the wizard in an attempt to prepare him for the quest at hand.

As the evening drew on, Kedrick got to know the old wizard quite well. He was loyal to the Queen, but one who would not accept the ridiculous behaviour of people. In fact, Asthal was exactly as he had imagined him to be, not a distant, powerful sorcerer, but a wise old man. His face was a roadmap of a long life, etched with a thousand fine lines around his kind, crinkling eyes. His beard was a cascade of silvery white, immaculately groomed, thanks to his magic spell. He moved with a quiet, unhurried grace, his movements deliberate and calm, as if every step was a carefully considered thought. Kedrick had noticed the small, telling details that painted the picture of the man. Even the way the wizard's hands, gnarled and spotted with age, handled fragile ancient books with a reverence that spoke of deep love. He saw the flicker of sorrow in his eyes when he spoke of the troubles facing Mantle, a sorrow that felt personal and heartfelt. Most of all, Kedrick felt a profound sense of trust in his presence. There was no pretence, no boastful display of power, just a deep-seated wisdom and an unwavering sense of duty that felt deeply tied to the Queen herself. It was clear that Asthal's loyalty wasn't just an allegiance, but a core part of his very being, a quiet, solid foundation in a world of chaos.

"Your quest starts tomorrow, Kedrick. Follow the candle to your quarters for the night! I will see you in the morning, Goodnight!" said the wizard as a floating candle blinked into existence in front of Kedrick at a single click of the wizard's fingers. The candle started to pull away. "Goodnight, Sir", said Kedrick as he turned and followed the candle out of the room and along the corridor, up a flight of stairs into a room. Every inch of the house oozed old knowledge, the books on the bookcases looked a hundred years old or more, and the furniture itself was exquisitely old with detailed carvings of ancient scenes.

The candle set itself down on a bedside cabinet next to a large four-poster bed. He imagined the old wizard must not receive too many visitors due to the fact that he lived in the middle of nowhere, yet the bedroom was sparklingly clean from what he could see by candlelight. There must be a spell on the room, just like his beard, he guessed, stopping the dust from building up on everything!

He changed and got into bed, which looked like it was going to be really hard, but when he rested on it, he found it to be unbelievably soft and comfortable. It was a comfort Kedrick hadn't felt in an age; in fact, he hadn't felt it since he was a child; it felt just like his childhood bed. His childhood bed had been so comfortable that he had never been able to find a bed to ever match it! Kedrick had just put it down to growing older, getting more aches and pains, but just like so much else that Kedrick thought he had known, now this little thought was called into question! Maybe the wise Asthal had put a clever spell on the bed? He didn't know, and quite frankly, right now he didn't care; he just liked it and was quickly fast asleep.

As Kedrick fell asleep in a comfortable bed, Captain Blade rode hard through the forest to the foothills of the Sunoon mountains, to his party of men who were awaiting his arrival. He had been riding hard for several hours, but now eased off as he spotted lights in the distance. "It couldn't be far now, that must be the enemy garrison base, where the lights are.", he thought as he trotted up as close as he dared to before dismounting and tying his horse to a tree. He continued on foot, keeping his head down and sticking to the shadows as any soldier closing in on his target would.

The enemy could be seen now, moving about their quarters clearly, so he looked about, wondering where his men were waiting. Then, as he looked behind, a bush shook, and then a whisper was heard, "Captain!" – He immediately identified the voice as Bill Brackets.

Bill quickly brought the captain up to speed; there were twelve creatures stationed at the garrison in addition to the five creatures that had kidnapped the Princess. She was being kept in the building on the left, and in the building on the right, half the Garrison slept. Beyond the building on the right, there was a barn where they kept the machine they rode. Bill had formulated a plan whilst awaiting the captain's return; he surmised that if they could disable their machine undetected, then a quick grab and run would work, as without their machine, the creatures would not be able to keep up with their horses. The captain agreed, "We will need to place men strategically close to the building on the right, ready to strike the guard and grab the princess once the signal is received that the machine is disabled. We will also need the horses to be ready, hidden in the forest to the right, to make our escape."

"Another man and I will disable the machine and then hoot like a Warbler owl to signal our success; there are no Warbler owls in this forest, so it will make a good signal", said Bill Bracket. "Very good, Bill, I need two men in the forest to the right with the horses ready to bring them out as we appear out of the building. Two others and I will rescue the Princess whilst the remainder of the men wait, ready to fight if the guard is alerted."

They swiftly moved into position; despite being made up of farmers and ex-soldiers, they moved like a well-oiled machine... There was a tense few moments as everyone awaited the signal, then it came "hoot – eler, hoot – eler!" The captain and his two men moved in; one man unlatched the back door and waited with it open a crack as the captain did the same with the front door. The captain was about to open the door fully and enter when one of the four creatures inside stood up and moved towards the window. "I heard something outside!" he grunted to the other creatures. "Ah – you hearing things again, you fool, Gluckell!", said another creature. This angered the first creature, and he raised his fist and struck the second down to the floor. The other two creatures then started shouting at the first two whilst pulling them apart from one another. This made the perfect diversion for the captain and the man at the back door to slip inside and hide in the shadows by the doors. "Hoot–elar, Hoot-elar!" was heard again, the creatures' ears stiffened, and their heads leaned to one side listening. That was the second sign; the first team had retreated back to the horses.

"That was an Owl Warbler", remarked one creature. "Don't be stupid", said another, "There are no Owl Warblers in this forest!" As the creature said that they looked at each other and the one nearest the back door raised his hand to the horn around his neck and in doing so signed his own death warrant as Janadu, who was hiding in the shadows by the back door struck him down before he could raise the alarm, making the captain leap forward sword swinging taking down the second of the creatures. A third man, Jenkins, entered behind the captain, and they both launched an attack on the two remaining creatures, while Janadu located and freed the Princess and led her through the back door and to the waiting horses. The third creature got in a lucky blow and killed Jenkins, leaving the captain on his own with the two creatures. He couldn't fight them both and was unable to stop one from picking up the horn and blowing it. Alarms sounded all over the garrison, and the captain swung his sword at the light hanging up, breaking the pottery container and allowing flaming oil to drip over the floor, which immediately caught alight between him and the creatures. He ran out of the door and jumped on a waiting horse, secure in the knowledge that the Princess had already made her escape with the other men.

The captain and Bill, who had hung on behind with a horse for him, made their escape under a rain of arrows. One struck Bill in the leg, but it didn't strike deeply, and they raced on away from the garrison. After an hour, they stopped so that Bill's leg could be tended, and then they rode on again. By morning, the nation of Thurk, a temporary refuge, was in sight.

Oblivious to the night-long activity of Captain Blade, Kedrick slept and dreamed about his mother. She had died when he was young, and he only barely remembered her during his wakeful hours, but at night, in his dreams, she was a vivid, living memory. She was tall, taller than he remembered, her form a gentle, reassuring presence in the swirling mists of his unconscious mind. Her hair, the same light brown as his own, was a loose cascade around her shoulders, catching a soft, internal light. The most striking thing, however, was her eyes. They held a profound kindness, a wellspring of love and worry that he felt deep in his soul. They were a warm, familiar brown, but in the dreams, they held a quiet, steady resolve, a strength he had forgotten she possessed. When she spoke, her voice was a melody he had long since lost, a low, melodic hum that soothed the ragged edges of his fears. She didn't speak in riddles or with grand pronouncements but with a simple, unwavering clarity that felt like home. But this dream was different to others he had experienced; his mother seemed lost to him. He could see her in a mist, but couldn't find her still. Every time he focused on her, she just slipped away into the mist to reappear moments later elsewhere, just to disappear again. Kedrick felt scared; unable to tell what was real, and he didn't know where he was! He could feel someone behind him, someone watching, but when he looked, no one was there apart from a tree! He turned back and sensed it again, someone's eyes boring deep into his soul. Again, he turned back, but only trees met his gaze. He started to run; he couldn't say what he was running from, but he knew he didn't like it! The land was semi-lit by the half-moon that was high in the sky. Shadows reigned supreme, but Kedrick managed to make out the shapes of trees and ditches as he ran. Then, suddenly, his desperate sprint was brought to an abrupt halt. He was faced with darkness, complete darkness. Right in front of him, he could still feel someone watching him. He was standing in moonlight, but directly in front of him, all light ceased to be, as if the world just didn't exist there, leaving a complete void of nothingness! Something changed; he took a step back. The darkness was advancing; he took another step back, and now, not only was it advancing, but it was flanking him, closing in on all sides. He was almost surrounded by the darkness now. With no option left, Kedrick turned around to run again, but as he turned, everything vanished into darkness. In a split second, he could see nothing; feel nothing, not even his own limbs, hands, nothing, not even any sense of breathing! Kedrick jumped awake, panting desperately, and dripping with sweat. Sitting up quickly in panic, he fell out of bed! Before gradually getting his breath back and climbing back onto the bed. Still feeling shaken up by that intense dream, but knowing there was a long journey ahead of him tomorrow and that he needed to get some rest, he took a drink of the water from his bedside locker and bravely settled himself back down to sleep.

When he awoke in the morning, there had been no more bad dreams, but that dream still sat uneasily in his subconscious, and it had done nothing to ease his concerns about what lay ahead of him.

At breakfast, Asthal relayed news that Captain Blade and his men had been successful in the rescue of the Princess and conveyed how even more important the quest was compared to the rescue of the Princess. "Your quest is to save us all and our way of life!" he told him, "You must succeed! I will use my magic to help you keep on track; if my powers allow, I will send a light to guide you". "How far must I travel today? The Great Lake of Misgiving just seems too far! I am afraid that I will lose my mind!" "It is not the distance you should concern yourself with, but you are correct about the effect the Plains of Confusion may have on your mind; you must stay focused on your purpose and travel fast. Don't stop for anything, not until you pass the foot of Einkwin! Not until then will your mind be safe."

The rest of breakfast passed in a worried silence, bar when the wise old wizard snagged his dangling sleeve on a nail, which had worked its way loose from the table over the past one hundred years, causing him to pour tea onto himself, all over his beard. "Dirty Cods water!" he muttered to himself, annoyed with the nail as the tea disappeared into thin air from his beard.

The wizard's apprentice, Grundlenut, handed Kedrick a packed rucksack as they walked to the front door. The wizard explained that the rucksack held everything that he would need on his quest, "There is even an enchanted Gelf Bag in there, which holds two slices of

Loaf!" "How is the Gelf Bag enchanted?", enquired Kedrick. "That is a matter of ancient Gelf magic, lost to time. But in practical terms, my young friend, when you empty the bag, it refills itself, so you have an endless supply of Loaf!" Kedrick thought to himself that such a bag would have been of great use to the miller who strived to produce enough quality flour to make Loaf at his bakery! "I know what you are thinking, Kedrick, but this Gelf Bag would be of no use to make loaf to sell as it will only produce enough Loaf for one person to eat each day!" The wise old wizard said, interrupting his thoughts.

# Kedrick Sets Out

Kedrick followed the rising sun as the wizard had told him, travelling directly east to the footbridge over the River Qualm. The forest was very thick; it was clear that no one ever travelled in this direction, and Kedrick knew only too well from Asthal's warnings and stories that he had heard back in Kevlar about the River Qualm and the Plains of Confusion.

He recalled the story of the old fisherman. The story said the old man had been fishing at the river for many years; it was known as the River Y Lli, which meant River of Life, when translated from the ancient words of a time long lost. Gevlings had once inhabited the land on the other side of the river, but things changed; gradually, the little people moved away, and then there were fewer and fewer fish in the river. Some argue that the fish population took a dive first, forcing them to move away as their main diet had been fish. But the old fisherman had continued to fish at the river, each day spending longer and longer there to catch enough fish to feed his family. His wife reported that he changed over that time. He started to forget the names of items like the salt pot at first, and then he struggled to remember the name of his wife, but not only did his memory change, but so did his temperament; he went from being a nice, patient man to being a bitter, angry man who hated himself and everyone else. And then one day, he never returned. Some say he threw himself in the river; others say he forgot everything and now roams the Plains of Confusion, existing by eating the berries of the no-no bush. No one in their right mind ever eats the berries of the no-no Bush, hence the name, as they give you an instant bellyache, and are guaranteed to cause you diarrhoea a couple of hours later. The thought that anyone would choose to live that way was crazy, but such is the effect the River and the Plains have on folk, and now Kedrick was on a quest that meant he had to cross those parts.

"OWW!" he shouted as a bramble found a home in his side, it felt like the trees were even trying to reason with him, by blocking his path more and more, they were trying to stop him from reaching the river maybe he thought, but then the path thinned out incredibly fast and even the trees stopped. He stepped out into the open, and he could see for a mile clear in front of him; not a single tree existed in front of him; they didn't want to be anywhere near the river.

As he moved forward away from the forest of Xendar, Kedrick felt uneasy, and his neck started to ache. He had felt uneasy about this journey before he had left the wise old wizard's house, but now he wondered if it was the poisoned land that was instilling this feeling. He knew he had to go on; everything depended on him, and he had to complete his quest for everyone's sake!

So, he swallowed his concerns and bravely marched forward. It wasn't long until the footbridge became evident in the distance, and a small course correction was needed to reach it, but Kedrick was impressed with himself that he had found it so easily. As he reached the River Qualm, his neck ache radiated into his head like a red-hot poker. He knew for sure now what was causing him the trouble. The river carried the poison that affected the land, and this is why his troubles had got worse by the riverside. The bridge looked like it would fall apart as soon as Kedrick stood upon it, but he knew turning back was out of the question and he wanted to get away from the river as soon as he could, so he ran across it without looking back and carried on running until he felt his headache ease a little, then he stopped and looked about taking in his whereabouts. To the distant left, he could see the proud mountain range of Ellowed jutting high into the sky. Asthal had told him not to wander any closer to the Lake of Misgiving or he would lose his mind for sure, so he carried on forward in a fast march, keeping the mountains at the same distance to his left.

It wasn't long until Kedrick got that familiar feeling from his dream that someone or something was following him, but every time he turned, nothing was there to meet his gaze. He guessed that he was starting to go paranoid; perhaps this was only the first of the delusions to come, he thought and quickened his march a little.

Suddenly, his right foot found a pothole in the ground, and he fell, surprised, to his knees. Fortunately, he was uninjured, but as he fell, he was positive he heard a scamper of feet behind him. He looked, but again, nothing was there. Turning to face front, a small building appeared in Kedrick's line of sight, slightly to the right. He knew Gevlings once inhabited these parts, but all had long gone. Maybe this was one of their houses, he thought as he got to his feet. The house stood alone with only a No-no Berry bush for company; it looked old and derelict to the point of near collapse. Kedrick walked over to it to investigate. He bent over and peered in through the open front door when a voice shouted," Get away from my house, you stinking crows' foot!" Kedrick looked around for the voice's owner but saw no one. "I mean you no harm! I am only passing through, I'm on a quest to the mountain range of Ellowed!" stated Kedrick to the mystery voice. "Then pass through away from my house or I will curse you, you stinking crows' foot!" retorted the mystery voice. "Ok! I will, I am sorry," Kedrick said, backing away from the house. "Are you a Gevling? I thought you had all moved away!" Suddenly, a sickly short figure appeared out of thin air in front of Kedrick, "What do you know about Gevlings, Crows foot? What have you done to my family? Where are they? What have you done to them?" The little figure was waving a stick in the air and looking very angry. "I haven't done anything to your family, I promise, I don't even know who you are!" "A crow foot's promise is worthless, worthless!" said the little person with the rage draining from his words as he said it. Kedrick noticed the solitary No-no Berry bush beside the house again and thought that this must be his only source of food! "Would you like some Gelf Loaf? I have some you can have if you would like," he said, reaching into his bag for some. He took the loaf, and as he ate, he seemed to become much more reasonable.

"I am the only Gevling left here! Everyone else left long ago!" he volunteered. "Why did they leave?" asked Kedrick. "The poison of the river, everything dies here", he answered. "But then, why did you stay?" As Kedrick asked this question, the round eyes of the strange little man held back tears. He had obviously touched a nerve with his last question. "My Gharmet and my Telulu are both lost to that River! I feel closer to them here!" "Others all left, but I won't leave my beloved Telulu and my Gharmet! They are here, you know; I can feel them watching me! The others said they drowned in the river, but I can feel them here, I tell you!" Kedrick judged that this sickly looking Gevling had been suffering the effects of the river's poison for quite some time and had developed substantial paranoia! Not wanting to upset him anymore, he changed the topic quickly, "You can have this Gelf bag, it's magical and produces Loaf!". "I know what a Gelf bag does, after all I am a Gevling!" retorted Flankell hastily, but after considering the offer using the best of his current faculties he added, "But thank you!" "You're welcome, I am passing through on my way to the Mountain Range of Ellowed and I am sure I will find more food on my way!", said Kedrick.

"If you see my Telulu or Gharmet, tell them I know they are watching me!" asked the strange, sad little man. "Of course, I will, what is your name?". "My name? My name is! My name is Flankell!" he answered.

Kedrick did not want to wait a moment longer in this wasteland; he feared the poison in everything here would get to him. He didn't want to end up like Flankell, sickly thin and paranoid, barely able to remember his own name! "I am Sir Kedrick, and I really must be on my way, Flankell. It was nice to meet you, and if I see Telulu or Gharmet, I will tell them you know. Goodbye!" "Goodbye, don't you forget to tell them now!" "I won't forget!" he answered over his shoulder as he walked off. "You had better not, I know Gelf magic of Old and I will curse you if you don't!"

Soon, Flankell's house had been left far behind, and the prevailing land offered no sight of an end. The ache in his head rang like a thousand bells, and he wanted to give up with every inch of his being! The poisoned land was starting to eat away at his resolve. With a flu-like headache and blurred vision, the only thing that drove him forward was the fire in his belly to save his homeland. Everyone was relying on him.

Kedrick hoped that he would soon pass the Foot of Einkwin, but he figured there was still a long way to go!

His headache was getting worse, his stomach was in knots with nausea, and his blurred vision had reached the stage where all he could see were faint outlines in a thick mist.

The air smelled toxic, and the ground was starting to get muddy under Kedrick's feet as he approached a stream. As he looked up and down the stream, he could see no bridge to cross it. Fearing his sight had got so bad that he would not see a bridge if there was one, he walked up and down looking closer in the hope of finding a crossing. He faintly saw a pole jutting about two feet out of the ground, not far in front of him. He walked over to it, thinking it may have once been a sign indicating a crossing point, and right he was. With the mist that covered his eyes, Kedrick could just about make out some stepping stones that he could use to cross the stream. They all looked quite safe as far as he could see. Kedrick's headache was so bad by now that he could only open his eyes a little, as the daylight was too dazzling and caused intense pain. He knew it was terribly dangerous to perform this crossing in his condition, but again, he reminded himself that there was no turning back; for everyone's sake, he must continue. He prodded the first stepping stone with his right foot, and it seemed stable. Time to commit, he thought to himself and stepped onto it. The stones were big enough to put both feet on. He stepped to the next one, and it too was stable. He stepped again, and although this stone moved a little under him, it held. Two stones in front of him, he noticed a broken one; it looked as though it would crumble with the faintest touch! There was no way it would take the weight of a man; he knew jumping the gap was the only way forward and sped up, placing one foot down on each of the two good steps and pushing off hard on the final one, launching himself airborne and trusting in his judgment, he committed himself fully! If he had misjudged the gap by the tiniest amount, it would end in disaster; he would be doomed, immersed in the waters of the stream, and all would be lost. The old Gods must have favoured Kedrick this day as his left leg came down squarely in the middle of the good stone. Still in quick motion, he regained control over his feet and stepped quickly over the remaining stones onto dry land, where he tripped over himself and fell hard to the ground. But that mattered not to him; he had crossed the stream! He got to his feet just as quickly as he had fallen, and with his head ringing and eyes squinting in pain, he started running once more in an attempt to get away from the stream's influence on the land and himself.

He fell over and over as he crossed the rough ground. Getting up time and time again, he carried on running until eventually he felt the throbbing of his head ease away to a dull ache, and he could manage to open his eyes fully again. Still living in a mist-covered world, he looked around, but couldn't see the mountains to his left! Was it possible that he had been turned around with all the running and falling over? After all, he hadn't been able to really see where he was going for some time! Straining to make out a landmark that would guide him, he saw nothing but mist. But then, faintly, what seemed to be a forest appeared in a break in the mist ahead of him! Kedrick prayed that his sight was coming back! Beyond the forest, Kedrick could now see a mountain! The only explanation was that he must have already passed the Foot of Einkwin and hadn't seen it, with his eyes only half open. He smiled to himself; he had completed the first part of the quest!

He started to walk towards the mountain he had seen. However, as he entered the forest, it grew darker as the tall, greedy trees stole nearly all of the sunlight! Very soon, Kedrick barely knew which way was up and down, never mind left or right. He recognised the bush he was passing to be one he had seen about ten minutes ago, which meant he was walking in circles, or was he? It all looked so similar anyway; it was hard to say.

He was ever so tired now, and thinking he was out of the Plains of Confusion, he decided to sit down for a minute and rest, just for a while to regain some of his energy. He closed his eyes. Just for a second, mind, he thought, and slipped into a dream world of talking trees.

"Lazy little Crows foot", said one tree to another. "Always resting on the job", replied another. "Meant to be on a quest, is he, a quest to sleep is all he's on", said the first tree." The trees then all laughed. A laughter that got louder and louder as more joined in, and the fun they poked at him grew! "BE SILENT!" shouted a woman's voice, and the trees all went quiet and pretended not to be alive. I know that voice, thought Kedrick, but his mind was too confused. He had been asleep for two hours and was intoxicated with the poison. "Who is it?" he asked himself. "I am your mother, Kedrick! You are on a quest", the figure told him. "A quest, yes to... to..." he tried to remember, but couldn't. "You must get up now, my son, and follow the light!" his mother commanded of him. The love and loyalty to his mother served him well as he got to his feet, even if a little unsteady, and looked for a light to follow, but there was none. He started to speak, "There is no...", his words were cut short by a bright light to his left. He turned to face the light and saw its true brilliance; it shone brighter and whiter than the sun, but it didn't hurt his eyes; it just felt warm, but not on his skin, in his soul. The light travelled back two or three feet and stopped. Like a parent helping their toddler take their first steps, it waited for him to respond in movement, and as he did, it travelled back another couple of feet and so on, until he was clear of the Forest. He could see the mountains of Ellowed high to his left now, but didn't realise it meant he was back on track. He just followed the light, but then he heard his mother speak to him once more in simple clarity, "You are safe now, my son!" The light then gradually faded away; in its path lay a big bridge full of pompous ceremonial carvings. Kedrick didn't fully know what he was doing now, but he felt, despite everything, that he must somehow cross the bridge and just keep walking! So, he did, his head was throbbing worse than ever, but he thought he was just ill and no longer understood the influence the poisonous landscape was having upon him. He fell to one knee at the highest midway point of the bridge and had to use every last inch of energy to get that leg back up straight and walking again, but he did it, and he carried on and on. The light appeared again briefly, this time in the distance, drawing him towards it.

Soon, he had passed the Foot of Einkwin, and despite still having no memory of his quest, he knew he had to find warmth and rest. So, on reaching a clearing, he searched for wood, lit a fire, and fell asleep next to it. Kedrick dreamed he was falling, or more specifically, that he felt he was falling; it felt as if his soul was protruding out of his skin, slipping forward out of his face, but it was being held back as if his skin was stretching with it. In truth, his body was recovering from the poison and cleansing his mind from it.

# The Elders Meet

Unbeknownst to Kedrick, whilst he slept recovering from his day's quest of crossing the Plains of Confusion, Asthal had convened a meeting with the council of the elders. It was with the Queen's consent, which was unusual, as the Queen was attending.

The Queen generally did not attend any meeting with the council of the elders, as frankly, they talked a lot of dribble, and their meetings would last for hours before an agreement on anything would ever be made. This was because they all thought they knew everything and were very wise, which, in fact, wasn't true at all.

The truth of it all was that the house of the elders had been started after a group of poor, long-suffering sons and daughters hit upon an idea to get their annoying elderly mums and dads out of their hair for a few hours each day! And it worked extremely well for the first couple of years, until one day when a leading dignitary from another land was on a guided tour with the Queen and other respected members of the city of Targon, they visited the house of the elders, because, to be plain, there was nothing much to see and they wanted to kill some time. It was the biggest mistake they could have made as the visiting dignitary mistook the elderly fools for a respected board after the Queen introduced them as some of their wise old ladies and men. Of course, the Queen did not want to look foolish in front of the dignitary and played along with his mistaken idea and thus created the council of the elders!

Since that fateful day, the elders had done nothing useful for the country at all; in fact, the only thing they seemed to do was cause trouble for people they had a grudge against or didn't understand. Like poor old wise Asthal. They banished him to the outskirts of the land just as soon as they had sufficient ammunition to throw at him. And they only did this because they were scared of him and what he could do to them if he wanted to.

"Do you know what he wants?" asked Gorem, the ugliest of the elderly men (and that isn't a reference to his looks). Gorem was a very good-looking man, but he was a nasty, twisted old man who, even in his youth, had been a figure of twisted charm. In his so-called "heyday", he had been a wealthy landowner with a face that could have belonged to a hero in a ballad. But beneath the handsome exterior, there was nothing but a hollow, barren soul. His fortune was not built on honest toil or noble deeds, but on a life of depravity and coercion. He had carved out his empire as a gangster, his elegant hands not calloused by hard work, but stained by the dirty dealings of a brutal underworld. His days were spent in the company of the worst sorts of humanity: hoodlums and cutthroats who did his bidding without question, and pirates with salt-crusted beards and empty eyes. He had been a man of dark alleys and whispered threats; a master of back-room deals that left honest folk ruined and broken. His wealth was a testament to his cruelty. Every coin in his bulging coffers represented a shattered life, a stolen dream, a family brought to its knees. He revelled in the suffering he caused, finding a sick satisfaction in the power he held over others. Most of the farms east of the river had belonged to him through one way or another. As he aged, he became less of a threat and focused more on income than on violence. Some of the farms were rented out, and the others, namely the farms that had better soil for crops and good production prospects, had farm managers employed by him to make him more money!

He really preferred to rent farms out because he would relish increasing the rent every quarter, to the point that he made an effort to physically be the one who visited the penniless farmers, who were struggling to earn a living with farms built on worthless soil, and break the news of yet another rent increase to them! Making money was not as important to Gorem as was the satisfaction he gained through screwing every last penny out of someone down on their luck.

But now the tide had turned on Gorem, as the blight came, hitting hardest on the east side of the river. His fortune had left him as every last one of his farms went bankrupt. And with it, so too did every last shred of decency.

Now he spent his free days away from the council inspecting carriages and carts for flaws in his self-elected role of transport inspectorate! Self-elected because it was a position the council created after a wheel broke from a cart and rolled over Gorem's foot! So, he had petitioned the council in his usual bullying manner to make changes in the law, to make cart owners pay compensation for such events.

It was a purely bureaucratic posting, for as everyone knew, carts and carriages did not need inspecting, as the owners of the said vehicles did not want them to fall apart any more than the layman. Sadly, the low quality of woodworkers that existed meant that carts did break down, wheels had a tendency to come loose and roll off, and no imposed fine for the event of them breaking down in a public place would possibly resolve the situation. A sensible decision would have been to establish a centralised woodworking college to develop and teach a higher quality of workmanship, but like I said, what interested Gorem was kicking people when they were down!

Betty looked at Gorem with the same contempt he had for her, "I don't know? Why would I? We all got the same invite, you miserable old blighter!" A term often used by the other elderly members of the council, partly because he was indeed miserable and also old, but they mainly liked to call him this because the blighter part reminded him of the blight that took his fortune away from him, and because his company within the council was so far from delightful, they liked to take every opportunity to rub it in.

"I just know I don't trust him one bit; he'd have us all in chains as soon as he talks to us! I tell you, no good will come of this meeting!" he complained. "Well, I wasn't happy that I couldn't finish my Wellington. After all, I have my daughter coming to stay tomorrow with her three boys, and we all know young boys have a good appetite. I thought I would cook a lovely beef Wellington to have for dinner tomorrow, but with all this about an urgent meeting with the wizard, I never even had time to finish my pastry! And I won't have time later, they will just have to have stew, it's as simple as that, and I blame that dangerous wizard!"

"Stop jibber jabbering, you two! This is a serious matter, having Asthal attending our council, we shall have to watch our step, especially as I hear the Queen will be in attendance too! I don't want any talk about hats, you hear, the past should remain in the past!" remarked Kendle, the former mayor of Kevlar, whose only reason for being in the council was that he couldn't cope with retirement!

He had led a busy life as mayor of the city; there was always something in need of attention, either the placing of flowers during a royal visit or the overseeing of Queen Dubark's fair taxes on trade. As mayor, he had often said that he looked forward to retirement so that he could take life more slowly, but once he retired, his new, much slower life did not agree with him. In the first week, he had rearranged the furniture in every room of his house at least twice and replanted the rhubarb patch in his back garden three times in an attempt to find the ideal place for it to grow! If this hadn't been enough, he had been painting the exterior of his house a different colour yet again when his neighbour, sick of the endless noise and paint fumes, suggested to him that he might like to join the council, at which point he left his painting and followed the lifeline to then council of the elders, where he was immediately chosen with his background to sit as head of the council. Since that day, he has never looked back, nor has he finished painting his house for the third time, and it still remains half yellow, half violet!

"Aye, we should refuse the meeting and petition Queen Dubark to stop all contact with the troublemaker!" said Sidney, who was now wondering why there was no reply from the other elders and why they were just staring at him, or staring past him. He turned around to see the wizard, Asthal, standing right behind him! It would serve him right if the wise old wizard had taken the fancy to turn him into a toad, for Sidney was a troublemaker of the first class.

Only earlier that day, he had measured the distance between his neighbour's potted flowers and the house number on their front door as he suspected they might come within one meter of the door number, which would mean the flowers contravened a law which stated nothing should be within one meter of the front door number on any house!

This rule had come about via the council of the elders, who had all been angry about not receiving their post on time because their letters had gone to the wrong house. For example, Betty, who lived at number 6 Creepers Lane, found all her post had been misdelivered to number 16, and the reason the postman gave was that the climbing ivy at number 16 blocked out the number one, so all he read was six! Each member of the council had a similar story, and that was all it took for them to decide to petition for a new law to keep door numbers clearly readable. So, Sidney had measured the distance between the flowers and the number and found to his pleasure that the distance was less than one meter. Then he took more pleasure in sitting in his front room, carefully watching next door. For he had given a report to the local Law Patrol officer, who promptly attended to enforce the law in respect of this allegation of illegal flowers. The Patrol Officer first measured them himself and then rectified the issue by snipping the heads off all the flowers!

Sidney backed away from the wizard like a rabbit from a fox. "Welcome to our Council, Sir", he uttered in cowardice.

Asthal grunted as he passed him as if to say, "You are not worthy of my words!" He walked over to the chairman's seat at the head of the oval table and sat down. Immediately upsetting Kendle, who was the chairman, but he chose to simply sit elsewhere rather than to raise any argument with him.

Half an hour went by, and not a word was spoken. Asthal just sat silently, staring down at the members of the council, and no one dared to say a word to him until Queen Dubark arrived.

Three members of the royal guard first entered the house and continued to look around for a second before two of them fell back against the inside wall with their hands on the hilts of their swords, ready for battle. The third guard went back out after ensuring there were no assassins or potential kidnappers hiding amongst the council. Then the Queen entered with the guard still on the lookout for trouble.

The meeting began, "I would like to start by thanking the council of the elders for allowing this meeting to be convened!" "Here, here!" cheered the council. "Also, to thank Asthal for taking the time to lay out his concerns for us!" The silence that followed said it all. The wizard was not liked.

"Thank you, Queen Dubark! I have called this meeting as the information I have been piecing together over the last few years since my banishment.", he paused for a second and looked at the elders; each one in turn, before continuing, "has led me to believe that the creature's, as they are known to us, have been undertaking some kind of activity that is poisoning the Great Lake of Misgiving."

He proposed that the Army of Targon march on uncharted territory with the intent of gathering evidence of wrongdoing and providing a strong offensive if need be.

The council of the elders agreed with him immediately, out of fear, but the Queen didn't. "Wise Asthal, I understand that you have gathered this information yourself, but I feel that there are holes in your information! I personally would like to see the creatures punished for the kidnapping of my daughter, the Princess. However, I do not want to send an army into unknown territory and start an all-out war with the creatures, without knowing exactly what is going on!"

He knew his intelligence had big holes in it, but felt sure that something dark was brewing in the unknown territory. "I assure you, the Army will be needed, your majesty. I can feel that something is going to happen soon!" "I have the greatest respect for you, but I cannot sanction sending the Army out to march on any territory based on a feeling! I am sorry, but I will agree to send a select few of the Royal Guard out on a fact-finding mission, and we can ready the Army and deploy them to the Forest of Xendar, in case they are needed." "I think I speak for the council of the elders as well as myself when I say that is a very wise decision and we agree with that course of action!" He looked to the council, who all nodded instantly in agreement with his words.

"Very good then, I will make the arrangements with Captain Blade and you, Asthal, on our return to the Palace, and this action can then get underway." The Queen arose from her seat, turned to the elders and said, "Thank you very much for your wise counsel in this matter and now I shall wish you all goodbye", and with that she walked out of the door, followed by Asthal, who too turned as if to say a farewell to the Elders, but instead gave them all a stern glance.

On the trip back to the Palace, the Queen and Asthal discussed Kedrick's quest and the finer points of the plan. It was agreed that the bulk of the Army would be deployed to three points in a line near his own house. Being under the cover of the forest, their massing would not be too easily picked up by the proposed enemy. Captain Blade was the Queen's first choice to lead the select team of the Royal Guard.

The wizard would meet up with the Royal Guard as they enter the unknown territory of the creatures, but first, he would return to his house to ascertain as much intel as he could magically. So, as they arrived at the Palace, the Queen summoned Asthal's steed to be brought forth from the royal stables and then bade him farewell. "I so hope all your misgivings are wrong, wise Asthal, but I trust your judgment implicitly and know in my heart of hearts that you will help us overcome the challenges that face us now. I wish you a safe journey." The wise old wizard mounted his horse, and looking back towards the Queen, replied, "I value greatly your trust and faith in my service, your majesty, farewell until we next meet", and with that he rode off into the dark.

Kedrick awoke feeling much more like himself; the headache was all but gone, and he could remember his own name and the details about his quest that had eluded him yesterday. He even remembered the Loaf magically produced by the Gelf bag! "At least that is breakfast sorted out!" he said out loud to himself as he reached for his rucksack. After rooting through the rucksack several times, Kedrick remembered the poorly looking Gelf he had come across like a misty vision in the back of his mind. "Oh, Yes! Flank...Flank....Flankell! That was his name. I gave him my Gelf Bag! Oh Well!" With that, he stood up, reached for his waterskin, a worn leather pouch that felt familiar and comforting in his hand. The Leather, softened by countless journeys, was cool and pliable to the touch, and he could feel the reassuring slosh of water within. He untied the stopper with a fumbling hand and raised the waterskin to his lips. The first gulp was a shock, cold and clear, a simple, perfect contrast to the heat of his dry throat. He drank deeply, the water coursing down his throat and instantly reviving him.

Looking around, he realised that he had, quite by accident, picked a particularly beautiful spot to spend the night; the leaves of the trees all looked bright and fresh like they had just sprouted out of the ground. Which, of course, they hadn't. The trees opened up to the left to give a fantastic view of the mountain range of Ellowed.

He knew the next task lay in the climbing of those mountains, just as soon as he reached them, that is. Getting to them was his first concern; he knew he had passed the foot of Einkwin and the Lake. After suffering so much confusion before, he didn't want to stray too close to the lake. Therefore, carrying on eastwards for a couple of miles before turning north towards the easternmost point of the mountain range seemed like the best idea.

And so, he started making his way through the whispering forest. The path was a winding, shadowed tunnel for the most part. Every step swallowed by the thick carpet of moss and fallen leaves, and the air, heavy with the scent of damp earth and decay, seemed to press in on him. The relentless, rustling whisper of the leaves above created a disorienting, endless murmur, a sound that made it impossible to tell one direction from another. Then, every now and then, for a precious, fleeting moment, a gap in the canopy would appear. A break in the leafy gloom would reveal a patch of sky, a sudden splash of brilliant, undeniable blue. In that instant, a wave of profound relief would wash over Kedrick. He'd tilt his head back, letting the sun's warm, embracing touch fall on his face, the sudden warmth a stark contrast to the forest's persistent chill. His eyes, quick to adjust, would snatch a glimpse of the sun's position. It was a moment of absolute clarity, a confirmation that the sun was still where it should be, a beacon of hope in the cast, confusing greenness. Then the moment would vanish as quickly as it had come, with the canopy closing once more with a soft rustle, plunging him back into the emerald twilight. But in that brief, brilliant flash, he had seen what he needed to see. His heart, which had been a nervous drum in his chest, would settle, and a surge of renewed purpose would propel him forward, knowing he was still on the right path, still moving east. Every tree looked like every other tree, so getting turned around and walking in circles could easily happen, but so far, he had managed to keep going in the right direction.

After two hours or so of walking, Kedrick figured he had travelled far enough east and turned north, putting the sun on his right side. The uncharted forest Kedrick was walking through had grown so thick that he could no longer make out the mountains, or anything else for that matter. All he could see was the thick undergrowth between the trees and the rare glittering rays of sunlight that sparkled through the forest canopy high above his head. This whispering forest, which had been a disorientating puzzle, now became a brutal physical opponent. For two agonising hours, the trees had grown closer, their branches intertwining into a choking thicket, their undergrowth a writhing mass of thorns and roots. His quest had devolved into a grim, relentless battle against the forest itself. His arms, once strong and eager, now burned with a deep, weary ache that seemed to emanate from the very marrow of his bones. His sword, the magnificent blade of Targon, was no longer a noble tool of battle, but a simple tool for clearing his path. Each slash, each downward stroke to sever a stubborn vine, fuelled a fiery protest from his muscles. The sweat, a constant, stinging presence, beaded on his forehead and nose, dripped into his eyes, blurring his vision as the insistent whisper of the leaves above seemed to mock his every laboured effort.

He pushed on, driven by a desperate hope that this green, suffocating wall would eventually break. And then, it did. With a final weary lunge, he hacked through a final cluster of clinging vines and stumbled forward. Before him, bathed in the soft, uninterrupted light of the late afternoon, lay a clearing. The sight of it was an emotional balm; a profound relief rang out deep in his soul. The air, no longer heavy with the scent of damp earth and decay, was fresh and sweet. The ground, blessedly free of thorny entanglements, was a soft carpet of verdant grass. He stood there for a long-enchanted moment, his chest heaving, his sword lowered, a monument of exhausted victory in a world of green. His whole body was relieved, and as his senses settled, he decided to take a well-earned rest.

Kedrick sat down on a tree stump, produced his waterskin, and took a drink. As he rested, a sudden gust of wind brought with it a smell so vile it seemed to curdle the air itself. It wasn't just a bad smell; it was an assault on the senses. The scent was a putrid mix, a truly wretched combination of rotting meat, stagnant water, and the pungent, chemical burn of something foul and skunk-like. It carried a greasy, sickly sweetness that caught in the back of his throat and made his stomach lurch. For a fleeting moment, the stench was so overpowering that it felt less like a smell and more like a physical presence, a miasma of decay and filth. Then, as quickly as it had arrived, the wind shifted, carrying the vile odour away, leaving behind only the lingering, unpleasant memory of its passing.

He had been climbing a gentle slope for the last hour and could see the climb was far from finished as the ground was still sloping up across the clearing and back into the densely overgrown forest. Densely overgrown, that is, except for one small footpath, trampled into the forest floor that lay ahead of Kedrick. A footpath trampled into the forest floor by someone! In fact, the clearing had been cut out as well, as evidenced by the slashed branches around Kedrick. Evidently, someone was here and had been for some time. He was too tired to cut his own path through the forest any longer. So, he continued his journey using the path in front of him, hoping anyone that he may encounter along the path would be friendly. Still having to cut his way through a little, as the path that had been hollowed out was only tall enough for a short person. Kedrick cleared a few branches out of his way as he walked, but that was easy going compared to before. The sun was directly above him as he made his way up the footpath. "Midday", he thought to himself as he heard a strange noise behind him, "fuloop!" He looked behind, wondering what that noise was, pausing for a moment with one hand holding the branch in front of him that he was about to swing his sword down on! He couldn't see anything behind him, and everything was quiet, so he turned to face forward and raised his sword in the air, ready to strike any combatant, when his gaze met the branch in his hand. A pair of big pink eyes looked straight at him, blinked with leaf-coloured eyelids, then turned away, as its tiny half-dog-half-frog-like body scampered away, fast, up and off the branch, disappearing into the dense forest! Kedrick let go of the branch and stepped back for a second, shaking off his meeting with one of the more strange-looking inhabitants of the forest, before continuing on his way.

Soon, the canopy opened up and brilliant sunlight filled the floor with a stunning visual array of flowers, brightly coloured grasses, and foliage. Having reached the top of the hill, the great poisonous lake was visible several miles to his left. Beyond the lake lay the mountains he wished to reach. As his gaze turned back to his path, he realised that it had not been a hill he had been climbing, but the outer rim of a volcanic crater! The remnants of what was once a volcano, long ago in the past of this mysterious land, the centre of the crater held a lake, which he figured should have been kept safe from the poison of the Great Lake thanks to the protective rim of the crater, sealing off this small ecosystem from its surroundings. That was great news for Kedrick as his water flask was running really low.

As he began his descent towards the water, his weariness began to melt away, replaced by a quiet sense of wonder. His gaze was drawn to a flash of brilliant colour. Tiny, vibrant red birds flitted from branch to branch, their bodies a stark, beautiful contrast to the green around them. With small, quick beaks, they chirped out a peculiar, high-pitched call, "eeeflooii, eeeflooii." But it was their wings that truly fascinated him. At the end of each wing, two straight, sharp claws extended, which they used with astonishing dexterity to scratch bark from fallen trees, revealing and then feasting on the insects hidden beneath.

Nearby, a different kind of life caught his eye. A small, squirrel-like creature scurried up a tree trunk, its long, floppy ears drooping comically. Its face, with its upturned muzzle, was fixed in what looked like a perpetual, joyful smile. Its eyes, dark and round, seemed to twinkle with a mischievous intelligence. As it scrambled and played, chasing its own tail and chattering happily, Kedrick couldn't help but let out a tired, genuine laugh. Was it possible, he pondered, as he watched the smiling creature, that the entire existence of these joyous little beings was simply to appear at this exact moment and lift his spirits, a small, much-needed gift from a kind and ancient world? The thought brought a warmth to his chest that had nothing to do with the sun and everything to do with hope.

Soon, he neared the bottom of the crater, and could hear what sounded like children. He ducked down into a crouch and listened... yes, it sounded like children. He gingerly arose and carried on, until a village of strange small huts came into sight and a very recognisable type of person, a Gelf! Had this been where all the Gevlings went when they abandoned their homes on the plains? But they looked so different to Flankell; they were much rounder, full-figured, and happy. Kedrick continued up to the village and introduced himself to the Gevlings, "Hello, I am Sir Kedrick of Kevlar. I am passing through on a mission from the Queen. May I fill my flask from your lake?" "We know of the Queen and your land, Sir Kedrick! We friends with your people, once lived alongside, before land fell ill and we forced leave our homeland and move here. Of course, drink from our lake!", announced an older Gelf. "Thank you, sir," said Kedrick, and he turned towards the lake and took a step, then turned back to face the Elder Gelf. "Can I just ask, do you know of a Gelf called Flankell? I met him on the plains on my way here?" The Elder's eyes opened wide, "Flankell, say you. Indeed I do!" He seemed rather taken aback by what Kedrick had asked. "Pray, tell me, how Flankell?" asked the Elder. "He is not well in himself, I have to report. He is very thin and confused. He says he stays on the Plains because he knows his Telulu and Gharmet are there," answered Kedrick. "Oh my, true it is, Flankell you have met. Oh dear! Refused he did, to come when left we did. because his wife and son in that river. They washed away, feared drowned! But when left, found them we did, wandering confused and hungry!"

The old Gelf had tears in his eyes, "Too scared we were, to go back. Poison affects us quickly. One brave Gevling, vowed return to him, but never heard again was he! So, we outlawed leaving the crater!" "So, what happened to Telulu and Gharmet? Are they here and are they ok?" asked Kedrick. "Yes, they both here, both fine. Poison wears off; takes couple of weeks. They both sad about Flankell left behind. We just not strong enough!" answered the Elder. "Well, the Queen said that the prophecy says that I will cure the land of this poison, so let's hope that I do!" said Kedrick. "I pray you do, Sir Kedrick. Us Gelfs miss homeland of plains. But how you cure land?" asked the Gelf. "I really don't know; I just know I have to travel to the tip of the highest mountain of the Ellowed Range!" "If anything we do to help, you ask." "Well, do you have any magical bags that produce Gelf's loaf? I did have one, but I left it with Flankell as he looked as though he needed it!" Kedrick asked. "We do. But is last we have, so you promise to take care of bag!" "I promise I will take care of it!" answered Kedrick. "Know I, your soul good. Late it is, Sir Kedrick. Think best stay you here, continue quest tomorrow! Fill flask, but careful be near lake; dangerous fish bite if close. Fill pouch from inlet. Is safe there, fish don't pass dam. Then we eat." "That is very generous of you." The Gevlings generosity soothed his road-worn soul.

After a simple meal and an introduction to their customs, he was shown to a small guest hut, a structure that was both strangely shaped and surprisingly comfortable. From the outside, it looked like an upside-down bell, its curving walls crafted from woven branches and dried mud. Inside, the space was small but cosy, with a thick bed of moss and a low carved table. A Gelf elder, with a soft voice, had offered a final piece of advice: "The lake's fish bite, at night, they crawl ashore." Kedrick, though weary, took the warning seriously. He latched his door firmly, ensuring a barrier between himself and the unknown.

Sleep, however, was not to be a quiet affair. He was Jolted awake by a rhythmic banging on his door, a series of hard, insistent knocks that sounded too close, too real. His first instinct, born of a lifetime of reflex, was to unlatch the door and investigate. But the elder's words echoed in his mind, and he stopped himself just in time. Instead, he crept to the window, a simple hole in the wall, and peered out. The path outside his hut was no longer a path; it was a slithering, shimmering river of life. Hundreds of large, sinuous fish, their bodies a glistening, scaly mass, were moving with a shocking, determined speed. They weren't swimming; they were walking on strong, bone-like fins, their lizard-like tails ending in a sharp, arrow-like point that looked dangerous. Along their backs ran a raised, spiky fin, giving them a menacing silhouette. But their heads were the most terrifying sight; they possessed a severe overbite of razor-sharp teeth, and their eyes, large and dark, stared into the night with a predatory intensity. A few of them, their forms thick with scales, thudded against his door, the same sound that had woken him. He watched, horrified, as they sniffed and scraped, clearly hunting for food. Watching the mass of fish pass, it occurred to Kedrick that the small lake could not possibly sustain such a large population. They must have evolved, he realised, to seek sustenance on land, under the cover of darkness, to protect their sensitive eyes from the sun. He pulled back from the window, the image of their teeth seared into his mind, and clung to the comforting thought of his securely latched door for the rest of the night, along with his sword. Just in case the latch failed. It also made him think about what other wild creatures he might come across on his journey to the cave of Ellowed. This time, the Gelf Elder had warned Kedrick, but when he was on his own, no one would be there to warn him of unseen dangers. On the other hand, if he doesn't get any sleep tonight, he thought, he simply won't be journeying anywhere tomorrow, and with that, he settled down for the rest of the night.

# Investigation Party

Asthal looked into the fountain of mist, and there he saw great machines levelling mountains and lots of smoke. An intense glow was coming from the mountain, like a fire, but far brighter, closer to that of the sun. Then he could see hundreds of fire machines, and the Army of Targon was in battle with them. The army was losing! Was this the future or just one possible future?

The fountain of mist always tended to give slightly vague information; the images the fountain displayed were meaningful but not literal and quite open to interpretation, but this time it seemed to send a rather clear vision: the creatures were doing something industrial that was hurting the land, and a great battle might ensue.

"There is no time to lose!" Asthal shouted to himself, stepped away from the fountain, hurried out of his study and quickly moved down the big, elegant staircase and out of the front door. The tranquil, mossy doorstep of the wizard's house was no longer a place of quiet welcome, but a launching pad for a desperate journey. His mind, a whirlwind of fragmented visions and half-heard whispers from his magical surveillance, raced with the terrifying certainty that the queen's army was about to be undone. His usual unhurried grace was replaced by a frantic, purposeful energy. He burst from the front door, the wooden portal swinging shut behind him with an unceremonious thud. "Grundlenut! My horse! Now!" he bellowed, his voice sharp with an urgency the apprentice had never heard before.

Grundlenut fumbled out of the house, his face pale with a mixture of fear and confusion. He saw the fire in his master's eyes, an intensity that burned away all pretence of a peaceful evening. Without a moment's hesitation, he scrambled towards the small stable behind the house, his boots slipping on the damp earth.

The wizard, meanwhile, was already in motion. He didn't wait idly; instead, he snatched a heavy leather satchel from a hook near the door, a satchel that was always packed in readiness for dire journeys. He checked its contents with quick, practised movements, his hands surprisingly steady despite the chaotic urgency of his mind.

Grundlenut returned moments later, breathless and a little wide-eyed, leading the wizard's magnificent warhorse. Its coat, the colour of a moonless night, seemed to radiate a nervous energy. Asthal grabbed the reins, his grip firm, and swung himself onto the horse's back with a speed that belied his age. Without a backwards glance, he spurred the steed forward. The horse, sensing its master's grave purpose, did not canter but plunged into an immediate, ground-eating gallop. The scent of enchanted blossoms and sweet night air was instantly replaced by the rush of wind, the rhythmic drumming of hooves, and the silent, desperate prayer of a wizard riding to avert a catastrophe as he rode hard to meet up with the elite guard. He had the distinct feeling that battle plans were already in motion in the unknown territory.

Quite some time had passed when the wise old wizard finally rendezvoused with Captain Blade, and his mind had somewhat calmed down and decided that scouting out the enemy first was the best way forward. So as planned, they rode on for Sunoon Mons, being most careful to avoid heavily used paths, not wanting to be discovered. They took a long and arduous route through it. Leaving the damp summer heat of the forest behind, the kind of heat that made the air hang heavy and thick, a soup of damp heat that clung to skin and clothes. The low rolling hills were a relentless sea of green, their slopes choked with thick, tangled vegetation and the incessant buzz of insects. Even on horseback, every step was a struggle. The elite guard, led by Captain Blade and Asthal, pushed their way through muddy ravines and over slick, moss-covered rocks. The only respite was the rare, cool breeze that carried with it the promise of the heights to come.

As they ascended, the landscape changed, shedding its lush green skin for one more of rock and cold. The air, once so humid and oppressive, grew clean and sharp, carrying with it a distinct chill that bit at their exposed skin. The easy, summer warmth was replaced by a biting cold that seeped into their very bones. The vibrant colours of the lowlands constantly gave way to a starker, more beautiful palette: deep greys of ancient stone, muted greens of alpine grasses, and the stark white of lingering snow patches. The ground became less muddy and more loose shale, a treacherous footing that forced them to ride with great care and measured steps.

By the time they were two-thirds of the way across the mountain range, the temperature had dropped severely; no longer were they basking in the summer heat, but freezing in what seemed to be a perpetual winter. Thankfully, they had thought ahead before setting out on this path, and all had packed thick coats to keep them from turning blue! The plan was for Asthal to use his mannequin spell to advise the Army of Targon to attack, as and if they found any activity warranting a military answer.

Before reaching the summit of Sunoon, they dismounted and tied up their horses, as horses had no place in the creature's culture, it would seem; there certainly had not been any reports of anyone ever seeing a creature on horseback! To aid the group in their reconnaissance, the wizard had come up with a crafty cloaking spell. It would not turn them invisible because, as he had previously explained to the other men, being invisible makes life far more difficult than being totally visible; as everyone walks into you, sits on you, and generally makes life difficult. Therefore, a clever disguise was a much better idea, and his careful incantation turned each of them into very hairy versions of themselves. Ultimately, making them look like they fit in perfectly.

Confidently disguised, they stepped out into the busy city of the creatures. In many ways, this city was much like that of Targon; there were traders lining the streets selling food, clothes and potions, the streets were cobbled to the same high standard as Targon's, and even the brickwork of the defensive walls matched the quality of Targon's. "How have they managed this level of workmanship?" asked Captain Blade. "Just because they look stupid, doesn't mean they are!" answered Asthal. "But the similarities that exist here with our great city of Targon do indeed raise more questions!" he added, sounding mystical, as if he knew the answer, but was going to wait for someone else to say it. "Let's continue on", commanded Captain Blade. Even the road layout matched Targon's, but the central difference was the Palace in the centre, or should I say the lack of a palace. Instead, in its place was a great big building that had a large chimney that billowed out so much smoke that it caused a dirty, thick smog to descend on the city. It was hard to breathe here and even harder to see, but around the large chimney, there appeared to be scaffolding, and from the scaffolding, Asthal could see legs dangling. Then he got a good look as a rogue gust of wind blew the smog away for a couple of seconds! There were huts built in the scaffolding around the chimney! "I guess they aren't cold there, at least!".

"True, but their chests will be worse than ever living around that chimney. I mean, it's bad enough here, not to mention there!" said Captain Blade.

"Well, we are not here to review their health. We have a mission to complete. I suggest that we make our way to the other side of the city whilst keeping our eyes and ears open for any significant information about invasion plans" The men all nodded in agreement with the wizard.

The magical disguise clung to them like a second skin, a heavy, ill-fitting coat of dense, dark hair that obscured their human forms. Under this illusion, the party, led by a watchful Captain Blade and an intensely focused Asthal, slipped past the large, dirty, highly occupied chimney; the group could feel the warmth given off by it and understood the desperate, impromptu dwellings of the poor that availed it. Not far past, on the other side of the chimney, a group of drunks stood bantering in gusto outside an Inn. Loud music played out through the entrance, but was only just about heard over the boisterous crowd inside. They passed by Captain Blade and Asthal, who had both come across creatures enough in the past to come to understand the strange dialect of the creatures' own language. It was like very broken Kevlarian, which to most made no sense at all. But after a little practice and a lot of patience, the duo had come to understand that the language was basically the same. So, they both heard a couple of creatures talking about their last night of freedom before they had to join the ranks of the Graigeth army tomorrow, ready for their marching orders! The captain and Asthal nodded at each other and headed past the two creatures into the Inn, followed by the rest of the group. They pushed open the heavy wooden door of the inn, the sudden noise of the establishment hitting them like a physical blow. The inn was a low-ceilinged, smoky den lit by the flickering glow of tallow candles. Creatures, their bodies covered in thick, dark fur, huddled in groups. Their low, guttural chattering filled the space.

They made their way to the bar and Asthal took a moment to oversee the actions of both customer and bar tender, observing especially the currency handed over – the coins they used looked very similar to their own but had a different figurehead on them, they had a king instead of a queen and he looked very like the legendary drawings of Ellowed! In very poor Graigish, the wizard ordered, "Five tankards of Flersch!" Flersch was the drink that the creature, whom he had observed, ordered. It looked and smelled like their own Grapft that was brewed at home from agricultural by-products. To everyone's relief, the Innkeeper nodded and quickly produced five tankards of the brew! "That be ten saply, please.", requested the Innkeeper, putting out his hand, gesturing for payment. The wizard then placed his hand into his pocket whilst whispering an unheard incantation under his breath to himself before magically retrieving the correct money from his pocket in payment to the Innkeeper's satisfaction.

The five men walked over to an empty table, sat down, and sampled the drinks. "Take your time drinking!" Captain Blade said to the younger men, who nodded their understanding. They sat back, sipped their Flersch, and listened. Occasionally, the captain and Asthal would crack a joke that they would all laugh at, in an attempt to fit in with the drunken, boisterous atmosphere.

By the time they had finished their drinks, they had gathered all the information they had hoped for! The army was to march tomorrow, and folk suspected it was going to be an all-out attack on the city of Targon and neighbouring towns and villages! It was the orders of the King alone that the attack be made, and it was rumoured that he was afraid that a great warrior from Targon would defeat him and take his throne!

They mocked their king, calling him The Scared King, who had inherited his position by being the last of a long line of descendants from the brave Ellowed! Asthal knew it; Ellowed had founded this city, which was why the architecture was so familiar, but how could he had he got it so wrong here! The current King was clearly disliked by all, having not done anything to help his people, who were all suffering with bad chests, but they feared his royal guard, who were extremely loyal and were treated so well by the King that they were ignorant of the suffering of the people under his harsh rule. They also mentioned that since the fourth crael plant came online, the air had got much worse outside the city too.

The group of men left the Inn and, once out of earshot of the locals, discussed what had been discovered and decided to head out of the city to see what else they could find out about the army's rendezvous site, which was reportedly outside the city walls and not far from the second and third crael plants.

As they walked, the creature's city, once a bustling, smoky hub of inebriated voices, slowly grew silent as the group ventured deeper into the residential quarter. The sounds of raucous laughter and guttural chatter faded behind them, replaced by a profound unsettling silence. The cobbled streets, which had been damp and slick near the inn, now felt cold under their feet, their surfaces catching the faint, sickly light of the moon. The houses were uniform and drab, built of the same darkened stone as the rest of the city, but their windows were no longer brightly lit. Instead, they were dark, lifeless squares that gave off an eerie sense of emptiness. A thick, oppressive smog, born from the ceaseless burning of crael at the city's giant chimney, hung in the air, a chocking, ever-present fog that tasted of ash and bitter metal.

This part of the city seemed still, almost dead, except for the noise that truly painted the city's grim reality. From every single window, from every dark doorway, came the same, wretched sound: a low, rattling cough. It was a sound that seemed to have no beginning or end, a continuous, collective exhalation of suffering. It was the sound of a city in pain, its inhabitants struggling for every breath in an air made toxic by their own industry.

As they passed the guardhouse on the far side of the city, they feared they would be stopped, but the guard just waved them on their way. Had they tried their luck at the front gates, it would have been a different matter, as the number of guards had been doubled as the King expected an attempt at infiltration from the enemy city of Targon. Asthal found a quiet place behind some trees, and whilst the other men of the team kept guard, he began the ritual spell to produce a mannequin, "Osra hat to deum, Osra hat to deum, myself to the power of two begin, Osra hat to deum, Invasion will come at noon, be ready, Osra hat to deum!" The full spell took him just five minutes to complete, and at the end, in a blinding light, a second Asthal stretched out from him as if he was being pulled into two. Then, as the second Asthal appeared, he walked off and disappeared into the forest, and I don't mean he was covered by the forest and darkness; I mean he vanished into thin air. The weakened wizard fell to the ground, obviously taken aback and tired from the spell. Captain Blade went to his aid and summoned another guardsman to help carry him to a nearby derelict farmhouse, where they waited for him to regain his strength enough to come to.

Captain Blade had witnessed the wise old wizard fall into this state once before, after a similar event had drained him of all his magic and left him very weak. He knew the wizard would eventually recover, but the other men in their group had never seen this before. They speculated whether the wizard had been poisoned by something or bitten by a deadly creature lurking in the darkness! "Our friend is weak from his conjuring right now. he will be fine. We must watch over him until he recovers, and then we will continue together!" Captain Blade said, reassuring the men.

Hour after hour passed, and Asthal showed no sign of recovering any time soon. Captain Blade paced back and forth, becoming more and more impatient. Eventually, he halted and stood still thinking, and then he announced to everyone, "We cannot wait any longer before continuing, but as he is still recovering, we will have to split into two groups. Teller will come with me, and we will continue investigating what is going on here, and you two stay with the wizard and protect him! Stay here until we return. We will try to find a way to sabotage the creature's attack plans. Remain alert, men!"

It was colder than ever now as the captain and Teller approached what appeared to be an adjoining plateau. In the dark, it looked like two more giant chimneys lay ahead. No wonder the air was so bad here, they thought; they had all seen the thick, choking smoke that billowed out of the one in the city centre, and here they had two more chimneys! Captain Blade shook his head in disagreement with the industrial nature of this nation. "How could they cause this pollution?" he wondered. But before he said anything out loud to Teller, he noticed something in the distance. With the chill wind biting at their faces, Teller and the captain crept along the edge of the plateau. Their reconnaissance mission had brought them to a bleak, desolate landscape of jagged rock and sparse, scrubby vegetation. To their right, nestled against the lower slope of the mountain, a scene of grim industry unfolded. Captain Blade, a silent shadow in the gloom, raised a hand and gestured, a sharp, decisive flick of the wrist, signalling for Teller to move closer, to take in the details. They hunkered down behind a low ridge; their eyes fixed on the spectacle. Huge, lumbering machines, painted in a dull, military grey, were at work. The drilling machines were immense, their colossal iron arms rising and falling with a slow, powerful rhythm, a deafening clang that fired iridescent sparks into the air that echoed across the barren landscape with each descent. Thick, greasy plumes of black smoke belched from the rear of the machines, presumably formed by the burning of crael to power such monstrous destruction. Next to them, smaller, but no less formidable, were the rock collection machines. These were squat, six-legged beasts of metal, with huge scoop-like attachments that clawed at the broken earth, gathering glowing chunks of rock with a grating, metallic shriek. They would hoist the debris into the gaping maws of a collection hopper, a final, guttural roar from the machine marking the completion of each task. It was a scene of unyielding, mechanical purpose, a grim testament to the enemy's resourcefulness, and a chilling sign of their intent to strip the mountain bare.

Suddenly, it hit Captain Blade, "That's it! The mountains are being drilled away to burn in the plants. We are standing on a plateau that was once a mountain!" he exclaimed.

They moved on carefully, and the air grew colder and stiller as they traversed the desolate plateau. The brutal clang of the machines faded behind them, replaced by a tense, heavy silence. They came to a final ridge, a jutting spine of rock that offered a perfect, if precarious, vantage point. Below them, nestled in a wide, flat basin, lay their objective.

It was the enemy's staging ground, a chilling spectacle of military precision and intent. A tall, jagged fence, a brutal line of sharp, black metal, ran around the perimeter, a stark declaration of ownership. Inside, the ground had been levelled into a vast, unforgiving parade ground, its surface of packed earth and gravel marred with the tracks of countless marching feet. A strange stillness hung over the area, a palpable sense of waiting. It wasn't empty, but full of a quiet, potent energy, like a predator holding its breath before a pounce. At the far end of the ground stood a squat, blocky headquarters building, its dark stone walls windowless and imposing. The building radiated an air of cold authority, its presence a promise of brutal command and ruthless efficiency. The only light came from a few flickering torches mounted on the fence posts, their flames casting long, dancing shadows across the ground that seemed to mimic the movements of parading soldiers. This was not just a camp; it was a cage, a place where a monstrous army would be born and unleashed upon the world, and looking at it, a profound sense of foreboding settled over both of them.

With nothing to sabotage and slow the attack, the captain decided to head back to Asthal and the others and get out of there as quickly as possible.

# The Quest Continues

"**K**reeelll .... Kreeeelll ....Kreee!" The birds' song praising the noble Kedrick was interrupted when a blunt object struck it on the head, startling it and causing it to fly away in haste, leaving a trail of loose feathers on the windowsill. All Kedrick had heard as he awoke was that damn bird again, once more disturbing his sleep by singing early in the morning! This time, it had proven too much for the tired young man to handle, and he had thrown something light at the open window, causing the startled bird to fly off.

"Ahh, awake you are, young Sir!" spoke the small voice of a Gelf Elder, sticking his head round the doorway. "This Toke, to you belong?" A cold wave of panic washed over him. The token, a small, worn piece of silver shaped like a winged horse, felt impossibly heavy in his palm. It was a lucky charm of the god Thersia, the god of travellers, but to Kedrick, it was everything else. The metal was cool to his touch, its surface worn smooth by years of worry and comfort. He ran his thumb over the faint, etched lines of the wings, and the world of the Gelf village faded away, replaced by a memory, as vivid and painful as if it had happened yesterday. He was seven years old, small and frightened. His mother's hands, so soft and warm, had been cupped around his. In her palm lay the small, silver token. Her eyes, filled with a profound and heartbreaking love, had looked into his, and she had told him, "Keep this with you always, my little adventurer. It will keep you safe." She had kissed his forehead, a soft, lingering touch that was a silent goodbye. That night, she had slipped away, leaving him with a memory and a promise. This token, a small piece of metal, was the last physical link he had to her, the final, tangible expression of her love. Holding it now, he felt the immense weight of that moment, a pain as sharp as it had been two decades ago. He clutched the charm, a single tear welled in his right eye, ready to trace a silent path down his cheek. He had thrown away not just a trinket, but the very last piece of her he had left. The fear, the grief, and the immeasurable love all rushed back, leaving him feeling shaken and raw. This wasn't just a charm; it was a part of his mother, a sliver of her soul, and holding it now, he felt her with him, guiding him, even as she had in his dreams.

He smiled at the Gelf Elder, thankful he had returned this valuable item. "Yes, it does. Thank you for returning it. It truly means a lot to me!"

"Come, for breakfast, join us, Young Sir!" invited the polite Elder. Kedrick got dressed and followed the Elder.

Breakfast was being held in a large hut; basically, it was another upside-down bell, just a much wider bell. "Sleep well, did you, young sir?" asked the Gelf elder, who had spoken to him last night. "Indeed, I did, at least until those night-crawling fish started banging against the door of my hut!". "Ah, yes, dangerous, they are. Now, see you, why don't get too close to lake!" said the elder.

The old Gelf turned towards a mother and son, and they both looked upon Kedrick as if he were the saviour, come to present them with the answer to their life's existence. It sent a shiver down his spine that they would behold him so, with such desperate eyes. The Gelf elder then looked at Kedrick and gestured towards them, "I introduce Telulu and Gharmet." Suddenly, he understood the look. She had the look of a wife who had just been told that her dead husband had been found alive, and the boy held a look of disbelief, the look of a boy who was struggling to come to terms with the notion that once again his father would play childhood games with him. Clearly, they had been told the news that Kedrick carried. "I am glad to meet you, Telulu. I must tell you that Flankell is still very much alive. I talked to him two days ago. He is a little confused and a bit thin, but he was asking after you. He told me to tell you, if I met you, that he knows you and Gharmet are alive."

Their faces lit up with happiness. In the little boy's eyes, he could see a flame starting to flicker alight once more as his mind took in the news, then as it sank in, and the flame grew, his eyes widened, and he could once more visualise being held by his father! Telulu,

147

who had been putting on a brave face for her son's benefit for such a long time now, could now let her true emotions rise to the surface and suddenly started crying as the months of believing Flankell was dead rose to the surface and erupted in what was now tears of happiness.

Kedrick felt slightly uncomfortable seeing her experiencing the rawness of those feelings for her long-lost husband. "I go, I must, to him; To Flankell, I must!" Telulu said to the Elders. "Cannot, Telulu. Too strong, poison is! You then be lost too!" a wise Elder told her, not wanting to see her throw her life away. "What for then, Flankell?"

Kedrick knew how dangerous the Plains of Confusion had become; he had only just managed to get away from them himself. For a Gelf of half his size and strength, such a journey would be an impossible task, so he faced her and said, "No one wants to see Flankell on his own. I tried to get him to join me and travel with me, but he wouldn't leave, so I left him a Gelf bag so that at least he could have some proper food rather than the no-no berries that he had been living off, so at least he has food now! I am on a quest to the Cave of Visions at the highest peak of the Ellowed range of mountains. Queen Dubark has ordered me to undertake this quest, as an old prophecy says that I am to travel to this cave, and that I will cure all our lands of this poison! If I am successful, it will be safe for all Gevlings to return to their homeland and rebuild it!"

"Good, that is, but how long this all take?" asked Telulu. "Well, it is one week's walk to the cave from here, I believe. Give me three weeks, and if by then the poison hasn't gone from the land, then I promise to go and get Flankell and bring him to you. He has survived a long time on his own with next to no food. Now that he has food, I am sure he will survive another three weeks!" Kedrick paused, giving her time to take in what he had said, then he asked her, "Do we have a deal, Telulu?" She looked up from the floor and met Kedrick's gaze and silently nodded. She then got up, followed closely by her son, and walked over to Kedrick, held him on his left arm and said, "Thank you for all you do for my Flankell." She then left the meeting.

"Good thing, you do. Saved her, did you! Thank you, wish to help you, we do. We, too, know prophecy of man who visit village. Prophecy say man, name of Ellowed, but you only hold mark of Ellowed." The elder said, looking at the medallion, "You not Ellowed, is you?" "No, it isn't, my family name is Wodelle!" answered Kedrick. "Strange, that is, but matter not." "Nothing mean a name, bar steps walked by ancestors!" said another elder. "Have Gelf bag for journey, also a vest made of Phantom Cat. Will guard you, it will, you warm, in mountains, it will keep!" said the Chief elder. "Thank you for your help. I feel more confident about my quest after meeting you all. After breakfast, I will continue on my journey!"

149

The elders and Kedrick had breakfast, Gurkey eggs, hogs' meat and loaf! The clever Gevlings had found that the eggs of a Gurkey taste absolutely delicious, but without the terrible Gurkey stench! So, they kept Gurkey outside of the village and the crater and just collected the eggs they laid. Kedrick had smelt the vile stench of the captive Gurkey when he rested at the clearing outside the crater, but of course, he did not realise this. It was a meal fit for a king and set him up for a long day's walk. He placed the gifted vest and Gelf bag in his rucksack and walked outside along with the elders.

As he began his climb up the inner slope of the ancient crater, the world of the Gevlings slowly receded behind him. The ground was steep, a mix of loose shale and stubborn alpine grasses, and with each upward step, the physical strain was a heavy reminder of his purpose. He paused for a moment, turning to look back at the village. The sight that greeted him stole his breath away. The entire village, it seemed, had come out to see him off. A sea of small, upturned faces watched him from below, their forms a tight, quiet cluster. There were no shouts, no grand farewells, just a simple, shared silence. The little, upside-down bell-shaped huts looked like a gathering of forgotten mushrooms in the valley, and the lake in the centre was a serene, shimmering blue, reflecting the morning sky. He waved goodbye, and the village erupted in cheers, which, after a moment of waving, put an extra bounce into Kedrick's footsteps as he turned away and once again fought his way up the side of the crater, only on the inside of it this time! Only just about getting out of earshot of the Gevlings, Kedrick found his passage so blocked that once again he had to rely upon his sword to slash his way through the densely grown forest.

At the top of the crater, the view indicated that only two or three more miles of Forest lay ahead of him before he would reach the edge of the mountain range. That alone gave his tired arms and aching neck a boost of energy, and as he rested for a second, he just eased his aching arms and neck. He heard a footstep behind him that made him jump, spinning around quickly, sword drawn, he found... nothing! "Must have been an animal running past in the undergrowth!" he told himself.

Descending the outside of the crater was much easier than climbing it, with the exception of a couple of slips on wet leaves, which, if anything, sped up his descent both times. On the last occasion, he slipped a good twenty feet before being snagged suddenly to a halt by a vine.

As Kedrick reached the furthest northerly point of the crater, his thoughts left his own trials. He wondered about the wise old wizard and how he had been concerned about an attack coming from unknown territory. He hoped that Asthal was wrong and that no such attack would happen.

Unbeknownst to him, however, plans of attack were indeed underway, ordered by the last descendant of Ellowed, the fiendish Driscol. Well, he called himself a descendant, but the bloodline between him and the Great Ellowed had become so diluted that Driscol had more goblin in him than the blood of Ellowed. Which, of course went part way to explaining the barbaric way that he cared for his people, the way he would sooner send his army out to fight than enter into negotiations with any neighbour and now his goblin heritage was showing again for not only did he have plans to attack Targon but he was putting them into action too by having the majority of his army report to headquarters ready for briefing and mobilisation.

Perhaps it was just as well that Kedrick did not know this information, as so much rested on the success of his quest; his particular burden was weight enough for him. Asthal had once said, "It is better not to know what you can't change!" Which, albeit, was not a saying that could always be applied to life in general, like, for example, there is no harm in knowing water is wet, despite the fact that you can't in any way, shape, or form encourage water to be anything other than wet, but in Kedrick's present situation, it was a particularly apt saying.

As our young hero slashed his way through his last few branches and brambles, he stopped for a second and, as he gazed up at the foothills lying in front of him, which, in itself, was a sign that he had already made ample progress today, he heard another noise behind him, but just as before. When he turned around, he found nothing stirring at all apart from some long grass dancing in the breeze. In front of him stood a green hill holding only a few trees standing tall. It greeted his glance and warmed his heart, knowing of the progress he had made so far today. He identified what seemed to be a cwm, situated high on the low mountain that rose above the surrounding hills. That is where I will rest tonight, he told himself firmly.

Onward he marched; he would rest before the mountain for lunch, but for now, marching on was the only way, and off he went under his own command, disciplining his legs to keep on moving at pace up the hill. His leg muscles strained and ached, but refused to quit under his determined command. He knew time was of the essence for everyone and that he was up for the task of marching at a pace. Of course, had he been less fit, he indeed would have taken it much easier, but years of agricultural activities like digging had strengthened his legs so that they obeyed him well, and his back was strong and sturdy from the bags of flour the miller had him carry about all the time. So, he knew he was capable and just carried on until midday, at which time he met the base of the mountain.

The valley that lay between the hills and the mountain had been tough to walk across partly due to the thick grasses that flourished there making every step a big step and partly due to the uneven terrain which had caught him out, as he had misplaced his left foot into a pothole, twisting his ankle slightly, causing him a great deal of pain. Kedrick had joked with himself, "A week with your foot up and you'll be right as rain!" He had said that out loud to himself, knowing that he had no choice but to carry on.

Standing at the base of the mountain, he put on his vest. He knew that as he clambered up the mountainside, it would grow colder, and falling foul of the cold temperature was not an option. Luckily, there was a freshwater stream running down the mountainside, passing by where he would be climbing, so if his flask emptied, he could refill it without worry, he thought to himself, as he eyed up the view and any possible challenges.

He ate a little loaf, had a drink, and as he lifted his flask skyward, he saw something high up flash past, flying at speed near the top of the mountain. "Oh no!" he exclaimed to himself in silence as he hugged the ground more, trying to blend into the long grasses by lying on his back and pulling them across him, leaving just enough room for him to see out. Then he saw it again, and confirmed his fears, it was a Giant Crascus, its body was at least three meters in length with a wingspan of twice that.

The giant bird was a predator that usually only grew to the size of a Goose at best, but there was one fabled and legendary species of Crascus long thought extinct, for there had been no reported sightings of a Giant

Crascus for such a long time, not for approximately two hundred years! It occurred to Kedrick as he ran over this information in his mind, as to why no one had made such reports, the Giant Crascus fed off the high mountain sides, picking off mountain boars and the likes straight off the mountain using their two giant clawed feet and then killing their prey with a neck-snapping bite in midair. They were rumoured to always make the killing bite in midair before flying back to their lair. Even if the animal was strong and could wriggle free of the bird's grip, once in midair, escape never served the animal well – so once the Crascus grabbed its prey, death was guaranteed either in midair or on the valley floor!

Kedrick quietened his mind as the giant predator flashed past again about one hundred feet up above him, just in case his thoughts themselves would give his location away to the terrifying bird. The Crascus applied its air brakes by turning its wings vertical and turned, circling above him, looking to the ground. It must have smelled me, he thought in quiet panic, slowing his breathing to shallow breaths and lying perfectly still. All the time, the bird circled closer to the spot where Kedrick lay, 'How can it see me?', he wondered. Not knowing that the creature's secret advantage was thermal vision, it could see the warm outline of Kedrick's body, or at least it would have done if he hadn't already had put on the vest the Gelf's had gifted him, it hid the heat signature from his torso, leaving only a faint impression of legs and arms that didn't show up to the beast, but his head did show up, thankfully, the heat signature of a head looked very similar to that of a bunny rabbit which wasn't considered as a worthy meal by the bird. However, the beast did smell something very worthy, something he hadn't smelled for an age, the smell of a nice, tasty human. A puzzled look was cast towards the spot Kedrick occupied, but there was only a bunny there???

The fantastic beast started to drop altitude, coming in for a closer look, determined to get to the bottom of this; it hated being confused. A rabbit was a rabbit, a boar was a boar, and a human was tasty! Kedrick's heart sped up as the beast descended, now only a measly fifty feet above his position. The bird's giant body and wingspan obscured the sun, casting a fatal shadow across the land. In panic, he moved his hand slowly to his swords hilt ready for a desperate fight to the death when the beasts head suddenly jolted up to the left and the creature took off like a bullet into the sky swooping down on to a boar that had lost its footing, and was stumbling and rolling down the mountainside squealing as it fell. Its worries would soon be over as the Crascus grasped it in mid-tumble and flew backwards away from the mountain, and high up over the valley floor, before, then lowering its head and with one bite, snapping the poor animal's neck instantly. The boar's life was over, and the giant beast turned and flew off down the valley and over a mountain at the far end of the valley, where it presumably had a lair.

Kedrick got to his feet and started climbing the mountainside as quickly as he could. He knew it was going to take some time, but right at this moment, the Crascus was happy; it was eating. Now was the best time to climb the open mountainside before the beast was hungry again. And then it occurred to Kedrick, what if the beast has nestlings that it has taken the food back to? That would mean it would be flying again soon! Back on the hunt!

He climbed faster, about as fast as anyone could, his ankle was killing him, but he knew that if he didn't get up the mountainside quickly and under cover, the beast would be killing him instead of his ankle, so he swallowed the pain and continued at full speed as if he didn't have a twisted ankle! He had to climb, and he had to climb faster than any man ever should. His body, a vessel of bone-deep exhaustion, was screaming in protest. His legs, once a source of strength, now felt like rubber, each push upward a shaky, uncertain tremor. His arms, too, were a battlefield of pain. His hands, torn and bleeding from grabbing at jagged rock and sharp edges, were proof of his frantic ascent. The raw sting of the cuts and scrapes was a constant, fiery presence, a pain he had to ignore.

The mountain itself was a sensory assault. The air grew thinner with every upward scramble, a cold, biting wind whipping at his face and making his eyes water. The scent of pine and rich earth of the lowlands was gone, replaced by the sterile, metallic smell of wet stone mixing with his own blood in the bitter cold. The loose shale and jagged rock under his desperate grip felt treacherous and unforgiving; one slip could very well bring his quest to a crashing end. He could hear the low, groaning sigh of the wind carving its way around the peaks, a sound that felt both ancient and ominous. It was a race against time, against his own failing body, and against the memory of a circling shadow that could, at any moment, return to claim its prize.

He had been climbing for an hour solid, and could barely feel his legs or arms, which was a blessing when it came to his swollen ankle. Nearing the top, there were a lot of craggy gaps in the mountainside here that he could fall into if he wasn't careful. He had no choice but to travel a little slower, as one injury was bad enough; he couldn't afford another.

Then, with a quick look round, as Kedrick had become akin to taking, due to his sensible paranoia that the beast would return for him, he spotted it. The Crascus, just coming into view over a far mountain. He had been right; it had come back for him. The tempting smell of the human had been too difficult to shake from his predatory mind, and even after devouring the wild boar, the bird's senses had remained too alive with the memory, and it had to return to find the nice, tasty human! As quickly as he could, he freed his sword and sank deep back into the nearest craggy gap, hoping the giant terrifying bird hadn't spotted him, but he was too late, the beast had indeed spotted Kedrick, before he had even turned round to look, and it was heading right for him now and it slammed down against the craggy gap, stretching deep with its legs, trying to get a claw into him. It couldn't reach with its claws, so it stood up beside the gap and thrust instead its long beak in. Stopping short, only about a cat's whisker in front of Kedrick. He was trapped now; he couldn't leave that spot until he saw the bird fly off with another boar, or some poor animal! He prayed for another animal to sacrifice itself for him. However, no other meal would suffice for the giant bird this time, and the beast kept attacking, trying to get its beak through a gap too small for it, but its persistence saw the rock starting to crumble and the gap widen. His heart was already in his mouth, and when he saw the gap starting to widen, he knew he must do something to defeat the bird and on the next attack with his heart pounding and the spirit upon him he thrust his sword hard and deep into the birds' head, the magical powers of the sword aided his fine ability with the sword and made light work of the killer bird, killing it instantly!

He was saved, he thought, but then as he retracted the sword and the bird's warm blood ran down his arm and across his chest, his whole body started to shake, and he began a second battle for survival with the beast! A toxin in the blood of the beast was acting upon Kedrick now. His arm and chest were tingling, and the sensation was spreading across his abdomen. Kedrick had no idea what was going on and thought the bird had managed to cut him before it died, he barely managed to lift his head up to look for the injury, but before he could take a good look his neck gave out on him and the second stage of the toxin attack kicked in as his arm, chest, abdomen and neck went numb and his breathing went so shallow, that every breath felt like it would be his last, the world around started to grow dim, draining somehow of light, colour and essence. The beast was staring right at him now, it eyes were open again and glowing with the darkest, most evil, red ever seen, it was staring right into his soul, then as the toxin took a full hold of his mind he felt the wretched steam of the birds breath on his face and the dark mass of the great beast raised up alive again and with its wings flapping, it flew back from the mountainside before coming back down suddenly squawking a loud high pitch squawk directly, right in Kedrick's face. He could feel his heart again, and it was beating extra fast. He knew the bird was going to get him for sure this time, and as the bird lunged with its head down to attack him, the semi-light of the world around him ebbed away, leaving only blackness.

In truth, Kedrick had passed out as the shallow breathing was starving him of oxygen, and the bird's rebirth had been nothing more than a vivid hallucination. He passed to an unconscious state as his body could no longer support a wakeful mode, as it fought to keep his organs from being destroyed as the toxin spread further through his body. Kedrick lay unconscious in the craggy gap for the next five hours, with only the warmth of the feathery beast keeping him from freezing.

When he finally came to from his ordeal, it had gone dark, and his head was pounding like it had before on the Plains of Confusion. He was confused and thought he saw a young boy standing in front of him! A boy with a face as indistinct as a reflection on a troubled lake moved in and out of his blurred vision. He struggled with his memories and strained hard to remember where he was and what had happened! Was he in the Gelf village? He remembered a boy, Gharmet, was it Gharmet? He knew the boy somehow, but couldn't remember how! As time ticked on Kedrick realised, he was paralysed, he couldn't move, but he saw the boy again, "Ok, are you, Sir Kedrick?" the boy asked, but Kedrick's lips would not respond, the boy held a large leaf above Kedrick and rung it hard so that every drop of juice from the leaf dripped upon him, his mind was overwhelmed in struggle and questioned whether this was some bizarre trick of his mind. "Feel better, soon, you will!" assured the boy! Yes, it was Gharmet, Kedrick remembered, but this isn't the Gelf Village, it's cold here and, and... a shiver ran down his back as he recalled the Crascus, the climb in haste and the battle that he had evidently survived. The world had dissolved into a haze of white-hot pain and a creeping, icy chill. He was only

161

vaguely aware of a change in his surroundings, a shift from the harsh, biting wind to a still, oppressive warmth. The metallic, bitter taste of the bird's poison was a fire in his veins, and his thoughts came in disjointed, broken fragments.

Through the fog of his semi-consciousness, he perceived the cave not with his eyes, but with a warped, internal sense. The very air around him felt thick and viscous, heavy with the smell of damp stone and something sweetly pungent, like rotting flowers. He could feel the cool, unforgiving surface of rock beneath his back, a solid, unmoving presence in his spinning world. Distorted echoes of water dripping somewhere deep within the cave's blackness sounded not like a gentle trickle, but like a slow, relentless tolling of a great bell to his struggling mind.

A figure stirred in the darkness, a boy, the boy. His presence was a quiet comfort, a small point of light in the overwhelming darkness of pain. He could feel the boy's hands, cool and soothing, a stark contrast to the burning in his own blood. It was a hallucinatory touch that felt both real and impossibly distant. He must have dragged him to this cave, a place of sanctuary from the storm outside. A place of shadows and distorted sounds, but also a prison of his own making, a liminal space between the agony of this waking world and the complete oblivion of unconsciousness.

Kedrick's lips started to twitch, followed by his right cheek, then his right eyelid. The feeling was starting to return; his nerves were coming back to life gradually. It was a miracle that he had survived the attack; only a few men before him had been exposed to the toxin of the Giant Crascus and survived, one man was Ellowed, who too had fallen fowl of the beast whilst exploring this mountain range and survived only by breaking a vile of Drakes essence over himself, before totally succumbing to the toxin. After his ordeal on the mountain and his triumphant return to Graigeth, the senate that existed back then declared the mountain range to be known as Ellowed's Mountain range.

As he recovered, the boy Gelf returned again, "You help my father, so I help you!" Taking a young boy with him on a journey of hardship sat uncomfortably with Kedrick, but he was here and had achieved so much to get this far unaided. Plus, he had certainly had a hand in saving Kedrick's life; in fact, taking the boy home would not only take too much time, but it might also be more dangerous than continuing on! "Ok, you can join me", he said, sitting up.

Much later he grew was concerned that perhaps more predators might be about and in a rare moment of genius he decided to make his way back down to where the deceased Giant Crascus lay and cut off a Crascus wing, the toxin coated feathers gave only a mild tingle as he touched them that soon went away, he had developed a stronger resistance to the toxin now. He dragged the wing up the twenty feet to the cave. He warned Gharmet to stay clear of the wing as it was covered in poison and left it at the entrance to the cave. Then, after having another bit of loaf and a sip from his flask, Kedrick settled down for some rest.

His plan worked better than he had hoped. As he slept, the smell of the Crascus nearby put off all smaller animals and predators from going near the area, as nothing was as deadly as a Giant Crascus; the smell of one put the fear into every beast. When I say there is nothing as deadly as a Giant Crascus, what I actually mean is there was nothing nearby as deadly as one. Whilst the Slesh Dragon was a creature of legend, an apex predator of such immense size and terrifying power that it is considered a myth by most. It is fabled to be ten times the size of a Giant Crassus, its body a colossal mass of overlapping scales the colour of obsidian, each one as large as a man's shield. Its hide is said to be impenetrable by any known weapon. Two vast, leathery wings, ragged and scarred, would span the heavens, and with each beat, they would create a storm of wind and dust that would destroy cities in an instant. Its head is a nightmare of bone and sharp angles, with eyes that glow with the fierce, cold light of a supernova.

In the morning, Kedrick woke and found a vicious phantom cat dead not far from him, in the mouth of the animal was a Crascus feather! After eating a bit of Loaf, he figured out that there must be a poison on the feathers that can knock out or kill someone. Looking around for his saviour, Gharmet, he found himself alone! Upon studying the tracks in and out of the cave, he realised that the appearance of the boy had been nothing more than a vivid hallucination. A feeling of loneliness descended upon him, but he was also grateful for the knowledge that little Gharmet was safe at home. There was a hard and dangerous task ahead of him: he decided that a few feathers might come in handy if he was attacked, so he grabbed a few and, after wrapping them up in leaves, he placed them safely in the bottom of his rucksack before he carried on with his quest.

# The Fallen

$A$s he crossed a mound the size of a small hill at the top of Gruber's pinnacle, memories of old stories told by Kedrick's mother flashed across his mind.

*"Never see a sight a sore as thee!*
*Winged Gods as tall as mountains*
*And mortal men as tall as trees!*
*Did battle high up for territory*
*With lines drawn to end their conquest*
*The men fought on to victory*
*They felled the gods like trees*
*Of the fifty who went up*
*Of them, who came down were only three!"*

It was, of course, the mythical story of a battle between man and the winged Gods of the mountains. The story told of how the winged Gods would come down from the mountains and kill men for fun, destroy villages and crops at will. Of how men got fed up with the Gods and declared war on them. It was decided by the Clan of the Grainers that all the clans should meet for an emergency summit to decide how the old clans of Mantle could make a stand against the winged Gods.

The Grainers had a vested interest in stopping the Gods because, like their name suggests, the Clan of the Grainers consisted entirely of grain farmers, and the Gods would regularly destroy their crops just before harvest, as if just to rub salt into the wounds. But the Grainers knew they could not take on the Gods with their lack of military knowledge and weapons. Therefore, they called out for all the clans to meet, and in an atmosphere of distrust, the very first all-clans summit took place.

None of the clans trusted each other, but they shared one common feeling: a deep disdain for the unfair and brutal punishments imposed by the Gods. They all understood that, if divided, no single clan could successfully stand against the Gods. So, uncomfortably, the talks progressed, with the odd slanderous outburst here, and the odd minor stabbing there. Such was their dislike of each other, but the elders of each clan enforced a tight leash on their younger clan members, and the hot-headed outbursts were quelled without further bloodshed, and no one died! Which was quite a feat in itself!

The clans, guided by their elders, came to the decision to hold a contest across all fifty clans to find the ten strongest men from each clan, and then the chosen ten would travel to the Palaestra in the mythical city of Galanthien to compete against each other to the death until only fifty men remained!

From the start of the Palantien Games each entrant was treated like a king until their demise arrived, and it was said that each brave soul who departed his mortal being during the games was remembered on a huge stone erected at the end of the games with the words "For the good of all Mantle we came and gladly surrendered our lives", inscribed above all 450 names!

All children are told this story, rooted in the living history of all Manthe, yet, to this day, the lost city of Galanthien has yet to be found. It is said the fifty men who survived the games stayed on at the Palaestra for the next six months, practising their fighting skills and growing stronger into an elite army of warriors. Until the winter fell, and they began their march to the mountains of the Gods. It was thought the gods disliked the cold and that it sapped their strength; hence, it had been decided to attack in the dead of winter, when the lakes were frozen and no creature stayed out in the open for any longer than necessary, for the fear of freezing solid. But, through this inhospitable climate, the greatest army of Mantle continued higher and higher into the mountains, to the land of the Gods, where they fought with the winged Gods for eleven days and eleven nights. Many men were slaughtered by the superior strength and size of their foe. But those that remained battled on, against ever-increasing odds, until the Gods became psyched out by the unrelenting attack the men threw at them, and not having any more spirit left in them, the winged Gods lay down and died together, beaten by the determination of man.

The men then built a large burial mound from rock and earth that took a further eleven days to build. It would stand over the Gods and the fallen heroes, to remind the people of Mantle forever that anything that seems impossible can be achieved by determination. The men who had survived numbered only three, and the story of their victory began the saying, "It only takes three Mantle men to fell a God!", which had been used ever since, when a battling group of men came up against unbeatable odds.

Kedrick now wondered if the gods had once been magnificent, winged creatures, their enormous forms soaring through the sky like living storms. He imagined their feathers shimmering with every hue of the iridescent spectrum, catching the light of the distant sun, twinkling like the stars they were said to embody. As he stood next to the burial mound, the air around him seemed to pulse with an ancient energy, awakening the echoes of a long-forgotten battle that reverberated through time.

In the distance, he could make out the Cave of Visions, where he was tasked with reaching. He could see it would take at least another two days to reach the cave. But, as he stood beside the mound, an unearthly connection was struck up. In his mind's eye, a scene materialised. The skies darkened as the massive wings of the gods swept overhead, casting colossal shadows over the battlefield. Their roars, like thunder, reverberated in his chest, sending shivers down his spine. Below them, the finest and most elite army ever assembled from the old clans pressed forward, their vibrant banners fluttering in the fierce winds. Clad in finely polished armour that glinted in the dim light, the warriors moved as one, a seamless wave of determination and skill, their eyes fierce with resolve. The clash of steel rang out like a symphony of destruction as the men battled against the towering divine beings. Swords collided with divine talons, creating sparks that burst like fireflies in the panorama of chaos. The scent of sweat mingled with the metallic tang of blood, filling the air with a visceral reminder of the struggle. Shouts of defiance and cries of anguish intertwined, creating a haunting melody that danced on the winds of the battlefield. Each movement of the soldiers was deliberate, a careful choreography honed through their harsh, unforgiving training. They lunged forward, dodging and weaving to escape the crushing strikes of the gods above, their training replacing fear with fierce bravery. It was a sight to behold, the powerful warriors, each an embodiment of their clan's heritage, fighting not just for glory but for survival against creatures of unimaginable power. Yet, as the battle raged on, Kedrick felt the weight of despair creeping in. Around him, he could hear the anguished cries of the fallen, both men and gods, mingling with the sounds of defeat. He found the entire scene quite unnerving, ghostly echoes of a struggle that had cost so many their lives. Driven by an instinctive impulse to escape the haunting memories, he hurried away from the mound, yearning for the solace of quieter paths, leaving behind the disturbed spirits of those who had once fought with courage against the heavens.

Kedrick focused on his breathing, trying to steady the rapid rhythm of his heart as he trudged through the increasing chill of the air. Each breath came in sharp gasps, a stark contrast to the steady pounding of his heart, an echo of the adrenaline that still coursed through his veins from his spectral interaction. The memory of the unseen enemy lingered in his mind, urging him to draw his sword and confront whatever phantom might be lurking nearby. His grip tightened around the hilt of his sword, but he resisted, knowing that panic would only hinder his progress. The urge to fight was strong, but he needed to stay focused. Instead, he concentrated on the crunch of leaves underfoot, grounding himself in the present moment.

As he pressed onward, he spotted a cave about a hundred feet down the hillside, its mouth partially hidden by a cluster of trees. This would provide much-needed shelter until the storm passed. The dark clouds above churned ominously, and small snowflakes began to flutter down, dusting the ground like confetti. Kedrick quickened his pace, adrenaline fuelling his legs as he navigated the uneven terrain. His heart raced with the urgency of his situation, the cave beckoning him closer. He took a moment to calm himself, inhaling deeply and feeling the cold air fill his lungs before releasing it slowly. Each breath steadied him, pushing aside the fear and anxiety. Determined, he turned toward the trees that would guide him down the slope to the cave. As he neared the entrance, the snow began to fall more heavily, swirling around him and creating a thick blanket over the earth. Kedrick felt his tension ease slightly; here was a refuge, a place to wait out the storm. He could almost sense the presence of the unseen enemy receding, a sense of purpose replacing his previous unease as he approached the shelter.

As the snow built up all around, Kedrick lit a meagre campfire and settled down next to this source of warmth to wait out the weather. Whilst foraging for firewood, Kedrick had decided it would be a great idea to grab a lot of the dry long grass that he had come across, and now he knew he had made the right choice as he lay down on a most comfortable bed of dry grass. Tomorrow, Kedrick would push on for the Cave of Visions again, but tonight, he would take a break and recuperate. He had a bite of Loaf and a drink of water, then, exhausted, fell asleep. Waking only a couple of times in the night as the fire started to die down, each time being disturbed by the lack of warmth. After throwing another log or two on the fire, he managed to nod off again in no time.

# The Loss

Asthal paced back and forth, "Where are they?" he asked out loud, not expecting any answer, as it wasn't a question he was asking, but his way of complaining about the length of time the captain and Teller had been missing. He was currently only so impatient as he had grave concerns over the disguise his clever spell had produced; not half an hour ago, he had noticed Private Chain's disguise flicker for a moment, revealing the true man that lay beneath. His mind ran over what could be done to stop any future flickers, and to be honest, he had come up with nothing, due to the nature of the spell, which determined that the spell couldn't be altered and would have to first wear off before a better spell could be placed.

The wise old wizard leaned closer to Captain Blade, his furrowed brow reflecting his deep concern. "Captain, I must express my unease about this spell's reliability," he said in a hushed tone, ensuring their conversation remained private. "I've observed Private Chain's disguise flicker, and I fear it may fail at a critical moment. We cannot afford any mistakes." Captain Blade, folding his arms, regarded the wizard with a mix of scepticism and determination. "I understand your worries, but we've trusted this spell before. It has served us well. Perhaps you just need to bolster the magic. Have you considered using an additional enhancement?" Asthal shook his head gravely. "Enhancements might help, but they won't address the root issue. The spell's foundation is unstable. What happens if the disguise falters in the midst of an encounter? Our mission could be jeopardised, and our men's lives are at stake." Blade leaned back, contemplating the implications. "You're right, the safety of our men is paramount. But if we depart at first light without a solid plan, we might be walking into even greater danger. What do you suggest?" Asthal deliberated for a moment before speaking with urgency. "We should leave before dawn, using the cover of darkness to slip away unnoticed. The further we get from here, the safer we'll be. It's a risk, but staying longer increases our chances of an encounter that could expose us." "That's a bold move," the captain replied, a fire igniting in his eyes. "But I see your point, if we are captured, we won't be able to sound the alarm." Asthal nodded vigorously. "Exactly. We need to make our escape. We cannot afford to let our concerns slow us down." "Then it's settled," Blade declared. "At first light, we'll be long gone."

With a shared sense of resolve, the two men understood that moving under the cloak of night offered their best chance of safety, ensuring that they would evade any threats lurking in the dawn's early light.

In short order, everyone started making their way back toward the city, and past the crael plants. They reached where they had left climbing ropes in place and started to climb. Their plan was working; the cover of darkness had permitted their withdrawal through the city undetected. The hardest part now was avoiding detection as they ascended the city wall by rope. Even though the wall was thick with soot, it was still light enough a colour for the small group to be quite visible to any guard who chanced a look in their direction. Asthal reached the top first, followed by Teller. As Private Chain reached the rope to start climbing there was a shout that came from fifty yards down the street and the local guardsman charged down on them to be met with the cold steel of Captain Blades sword, but the commotion had alert other guards and the captain had to fight off another three guards whilst Private Chain made his escape, then Captain Blade took his turn at the rope climb. He was almost at the top, and Teller was reaching out his hand to the captain, when a whistling noise flew through the air, and an arrow struck the good captain in the back. Teller knew the captain would not make it, "GO.....goooo!" said the captain with little energy. He lifted back and wrapped the rope around his wrist and drew his sword high, shouting, "For Queen and Targon!!" as two more arrows struck him in the back and his soul fell from his body just as quickly as the sword fell from his lifeless hand. The brave captain was dead. But his final act of distraction had given

Teller and the others just enough time to get away, and they raced like madmen down the mountainous path to the forest that lay beneath and across the forest to the army waiting for them. "The enemy is coming. We must win this battle, Targon demands it!". Said Teller.

"Where is Captain Blade? Queen Dubark ordered me to take my briefing from him?" asked General Station, a high-ranking general of Queen Dubark's Army.

"Captain Blade was killed during our escape from the city of Graigeth. He saved our lives!" Answered Asthal. "But now you must listen to us, the enemy is coming, the alarm has been raised, and it won't be long before they are upon us!", "Don't worry, sir", interrupted the General, just as Asthal was going to point out that out flanking the enemy would be the best defence, "I have two hundred men posted to the trees either side of the opening of the mountain and when the enemy come through we will first deploy the front line of troops here to stand and face them, but once the enemy have all come past my men the two flanks will cut off their escape and they will have no choice but to surrender or die."

Under the general's watchful command, all the men took cover, waiting for the enemy to appear. The general frequently checked on the positions of his soldiers, while Asthal murmured to himself, trying to recall an old spell. "By the ancient winds, grant me strength," he whispered. "With the light of the stars, I call upon your magic." His brow furrowed in concentration as he continued, "Memory of ages past, awaken within me." Despite the tension in the air, his focus remained on the words he had nearly forgotten.

At that moment, everyone heard a roar of shouting, and the enemy appeared from the mouth of the mountains, charging right for the visible line of Queen Dubark's Army.

The Queen's finest archers, who were nestled quietly in the tree lines to the left and the right, held their nerves as the enemy advanced between them. Every part of them ached to let fly their arrows, but they were highly trained and knew they must wait for the command. For each and every archer, time passed slowly, and seconds felt like dragged-out minutes whilst they waited, and waited for that lethal command to arrive. Then, finally, the order came, "Archers; Take Aim; Fire!" Finally, came the order.

Arrows flew through the air into the charging column of the enemy. Taken by surprise, many fell to the ground dead and dying from mortal strikes; others lay injured, bleeding out, but not fatally, yet, unable to continue! But still a large group remained, now running at full speed for the visible line of Queen Dubark's Army. "Front lines, Charge!" sounded the General, and the front three lines of the Queen's Army charged forward at the enemy! With spears firmly held out, the two armies slammed into each other, and a loud splintering of wood was heard that foretold the deaths of at least two dozen men and creatures. Hand-to-hand combat had begun, and the blood spilt like wine onto the floor as creature after creature received fatal blows from swords and axes. Amidst the death toll and acrid smell of blood, much like any battle, no one seemed to be really winning.

A horn sounded in the distance, and a second column of creatures charged forward onto the battlefield. They were better armoured and sported swords rather than axes, an indication that they had received better training, and would be harder to put down. And indeed, as this final column of creatures passed the hidden archers, where their predecessors had been struck down, obeying the shouted orders of their commander from the front, they raised their shields above their heads, interlocking them with one another! Whilst they continually charged onward into battle. The arrows struck only their shields, not taking a single life, splintering away broken and worthless. But as the rain of arrows lifted, a further order from the General suddenly changed the odds back in favour of the Queen's Army, "Cavalry Charge!" And with that, one hundred men on armoured horses entered the battle! Fifty entered from the rear right, charging across the rear of the last column, striking down creatures with every swing of their swords, whilst, simultaneously, fifty entered from the left, bringing the same devastating attack to the column's right-hand side. Cutting across the front of the column with swords, still swinging, they slew every single creature they crossed without mercy, effectively bringing the column to a halt.

A further rain of arrows flooded the sky. This time, the creatures were unprepared after the cavalry attack, and many of the creatures in the back rows of the enemy column fell to the ground. But such was the training of this regiment, the remaining creatures did not falter from their path, and in consequence, the battle was not over as the enemy army charged forward on Queen Dubark's front line. The loss of life on both sides was horrific as creatures fought men and men fought creatures, to the death.

Then, as the carnage continued on this, most bloody of grounds, a further trumpet blow from the Generals command, saw half of the Queens Cavalry detachment charge in at the enemies rear rows from the left swinging their swords and taking no hostages, then just as the cavalry cleared the enemies ranks to the right a further blew on the trumpet signalled the second half of the detachment to start their run from the right attacking the front line of the enemy. At which point, Asthal's incantation finally gave life to a life-size illusion of a Sleth Dragon right in front of the troops, and as the dragon spat imaginary fire out of its mouth onto the ground, it created a mind-blowing illusion that not one of the creatures questioned. The creatures, then in fear of the Sleth Dragon, turned back to run and faced the archers, who stood with bows and arrows at the ready, and the full Cavalry detachment, with swords held at the ready for another attack. Almost instantaneously, the whole of the remaining Graigeth Army kneeled and placed their weapons on the ground in front of them, surrendering to an army that appeared to have a Slesh Dragon as a formidable part of its ranks.

# Cave of Visions

Kedrick dreamt of his life back home when he was a boy. His father had taken him out, away from his home in Thurk. As a treat, they had spent the day fishing off the coast of Kevlar with some of their father's friends. It had been snowing that day, and as Kedrick slept, his mind circled all the events of the day, the boat, his fishing rod in hand and a smile on his face. Close to the land the water had already begun to freeze, and he could even feel the crunch of fresh fallen snow under his boots as he followed the men carrying their boat over the ice to the water, but they were quite happy having to undergo this extra chore as the fish swimming off the coast of Kevlar, in winter, were twice the size of the fish that inhabited the waters during the warmer months. Kedrick had never been fishing before, and everything that could go wrong for him had already happened. He had dropped the bait over the side of the boat five times, whilst trying to secure it to his hook; he had knocked over his father's flask of Tae and had stood on one of his father's friend's best boxes of flies! But no one was upset with Kedrick; they all accepted the mishaps for what they were, little accidents without any malicious intent, and they just smiled at Kedrick. He had been surprised that such bulky men, who had built up their muscles from long hours of fishing, in the worst weathers imaginable, could be so forgiving. That day, Kedrick had caught a whopper of a fish, the biggest of the day, well, technically, Kedrick's father reeled the fish in, but it had bitten Kedrick's Fishing rod. Oddly, it was the accidental dropping of bait over the side that had helped to snare this particular large and hungry fish, it had been passing by under the boat, well beneath the hooks and lines of the men, when a tasty morsel bounced off what could only be described as a nose, it smelt nice and tasted even better than it smelt, the large fish circled a bit and not before long was rewarded for its patience by another juicy morsel, which it snapped up in one bite. Now the fish was getting greedy, it figured it was quite a way from the men's lines and swam up a little and waited to see if any more rewards would come its way and right enough, another juicy morsel floated down to it. Snap went his mouth again, and the morsel was gone; the fish swam further up again and again was rewarded by another morsel of food. The fish had started to lose control, now thinking he was on to a good thing, he swam a little further up, nearly level with the lines, and another juicy morsel fell his way, snap his mouth went again, he surely was a lucky Galgahern fish he thought and swam up, just under the boat, the source of his new nutrition, waiting for his feed, and then it came and snap his mouth went once more, but this time he also felt an intolerable pain of a hook being snared in through his mouth. How could I have been so stupid, he thought! I've spent years swimming slightly lower in the water than the other fish to avoid the lines that they never came back from, and now I, too, am hooked! He flipped and he flopped with all his might, he pulled and pulled away from the line, but it wouldn't release him. In fact, the more he struggled, the firmer the hook lodged in him, yet he kept on trying and trying to escape. He felt himself being pulled through the water against his will, despite his fighting, and before long, he was breathing his last breaths as he left the water and flew through the air towards the men. Kedrick had never thought about the struggle with life the fish had gone through that day; he only knew of the warm companionship of his father and his father's friends, who had all heralded Kedrick as the day's best fisherman. Long gone were those days, and as Kedrick awoke, he returned to the harsh reality of his current situation, all alone in a cave amidst the mountains. Yet there was solace to be had in the fact that his quest would soon be over, as he was not too far from the Cave of Visions, just another day's journey, and he should reach it. Hopefully, before nightfall. With that in mind, Kedrick woke himself up properly and had a bit more Loaf from the Gelf bag. By now, he was getting rather sick of just eating Loaf; it satisfied his hunger, but not his taste buds! "When all this questing is over, I certainly won't be going back to work for the miller, I don't think I will be able to look at another slice of Loaf for as long as I live!" he said out loud to himself.

Walking again, Kedrick kept the morning sun to his back now as he was heading due west. Looking up to the mountain that lay ahead of him, he could see a small bump on the top, which he thought must be the cave. There seemed to be a winding path up the mountain, but Kedrick was too far away to tell if it was a path or just some natural formation of rocks. Before reaching the mountain, he would have to first make his way to the valley floor, and with a heavily forested section coming up, he couldn't actually see the base of the mountain! All he could do was watch his step and take his time as there were vines growing across the floor of the sloping forest, hidden by the snow, making it too easy to trip. After an hour of careful trudging through the snow, the ground started to level out. Then out of the blue, Kedrick came up to a sheer drop, a sheer drop of at least five hundred feet or more; in fact, Kedrick could not see anything below apart from blackness! Ahead of him was the base of the mountain he wanted to climb, but the ravine that he stood on the edge of was at least fifty feet wide! He wondered how he could possibly cross the ravine; he had no rope or grappling hook, but there must be some way. He dug around his feet and picked up the end of one of the vines, and gave it a tug to see how strong it was. It seemed strong enough; maybe he could make use of the vines that had caused him so much work over the last hour! As he stood and stared blankly along the ravine, trying to figure out how to make a grappling hook, Kedrick's gaze was drawn to a bridge in the distance. He walked over to investigate and found a stone bridge, beautifully crafted, spanning the ravine in a graceful arc. Small pillars lined either side, serving as a safety rail. Just as he was about to step onto the bridge, the mist shifted to the right, revealing a second bridge. This one was equally stunning, but Kedrick could only see the first half of it. Then, just as suddenly as it had appeared, the mist quickly cloaked the rest, leaving him with a fleeting glimpse of its beauty before it disappeared. Kedrick wondered where that bridge might lead, what adventures might lie ahead of it. That would have to be an adventure for another day, he told himself as he firmly stepped forward onto the bridge that lay at his feet. The bridge looked as old as the mountains, but it was strong, and Kedrick had no concerns over crossing it. Even with the vines that had themselves crossed the bridge, weaving in and out of the tiny pillars, it still looked good and solid. Once across, Kedrick wasted no time making his way to the base of the mountain and began climbing. He wanted to know what lay ahead of him in the Cave of Visions. His curiosity infused him, making climbing the steep mountainside easier. Not long after, Kedrick stumbled onto what was indeed a winding path running up and around the mountainside. It made life a lot easier; before, he had been grabbing at exposed tree roots with his still sore hands and avoiding collapsing rocks that rolled away under his step. Now all he had to do was walk. True, he had twice as far to travel this way, but it would take him less than half the time.

The day drew on, and Kedrick had been walking the path for many hours and was now quite close to the top. As he looked down, he could see that this truly was the highest mountain in the range, towering above all others. The peak was not far ahead of him now; it lay just above, hidden in a misty cloud that had started to descend the mountain. A few minutes and a couple of hundred footsteps later, Kedrick was now surrounded by a thick fog. The fog was so thick that he could not even see his hand held at arm's length in front of him, yet he continued very carefully, feeling the floor with his feet as he moved. Soon, he was too close to the edge of the path and about to take a step when a brilliant, blinding light shone to his left out of nowhere. He withdrew his foot and turned to the left, almost instinctively following the light. He felt his way toward the light with his feet, checking for stable ground under them at all times, but the light kept moving away from him. Kedrick didn't realise it, but the light had been manifested by Asthal, who had received a sudden sense of doom surrounding Kedrick, who had been about to step off the edge of the path and fall down the mountain. The light had saved him and was now guiding him along, on the correct path as Asthal had promised.

The light led Kedrick onto flat ground at the top of the mountain, "This is it", he thought, "I am at the top!" The light pulled him further forward to a point, and then it diminished. As the light dissipated in front of him, he was able to make out a solid object in front of him. Kedrick examined the table, feeling its rough, rock-like surface. In the centre of the table, he noticed a slot. But what was its purpose? Suddenly, it struck him, the sword he carried would fit perfectly into that slot. He fumbled for the sword at his hip, unsheathed it, and carefully positioned it over the slot. As the sword struck the bottom, a clicking sound echoed through the cave, and suddenly, the entire space was illuminated. Magical lights glimmered, leading into a tunnel.

Kedrick knew he had to follow the lights, but a wave of reluctance washed over him. He didn't want to leave the sword behind; it had been entrusted to him and was a relic from a bygone era, a valuable piece of history. He attempted to retrieve the sword from the stone table, but it wouldn't budge. Something had locked it securely in place! Begrudgingly, Kedrick left the sword and walked into the tunnel. The lights were very strange, enclosed in some kind of clear pottery that he had never seen before, but not only did this new type of pottery bemuse Kedrick, so did the cold flameless light that illuminated everything from behind the pottery! Was it a trapped soul made to do the bidding of the cave? There was so much Kedrick didn't know as he walked down the tunnel. One thing was certain: upon leaving the

Cave of Visions, he would never look upon his world in the same way ever again.

Kedrick reached the end of the tunnel and entered a small, dark, unlit chamber that felt magical. The feeling felt like the sense of freshness you get next to a waterfall; there was something in the air that made his body feel awake, even his nose was alive, feeling the air he was breathing more than usual. The chamber lit up, just as the tunnel had before, illuminating a stone crucible at the far end of the chamber. Kedrick walked over to it. In the crucible was the same clear pottery. As he looked around the chamber, he wondered what else might be present. After all, he was supposed to receive a vision here that would change the world and heal the land from its poison, wasn't he? Yet, there was nothing else in the chamber, only the crucible with its clear pottery. Despite his efforts, nothing happened at all. Kedrick stood and stared at the crucible, willing it to come to life, desperately hoping for something magical to occur, but there was only silence. He began to feel that his quest and the historical prophecy were nothing more than a waste of time. Feeling defeated by this anticlimactic turn of events after the hardships he had endured over the past week, he sat down on the floor, his spirits low.

With his head hanging down, Kedrick was on the verge of giving up and contemplating his journey back home. Yet, deep inside, a spark of positivity remained alive. He thought, "This can't be all there is; there has to be something more, something I've missed." This hope ignited a determination within him, nudging him to reconsider what he might have overlooked. Then, when he raised his head a little, he noticed a recess in the wall beside the crucible; in fact, it wasn't just a recess; it was a recess in the shape of Kedrick's medallion! Is this why his family had looked after the medallion and passed it down from father to son for so many years? Had Ellowed built this crucible? Or had Ellowed just stumbled upon the medallion and the sword? There is only one way to know the answers he guessed, and he removed the medallion from his neck and pressed it into the recess. Again, he heard a click as the medallion locked in place. There was a loud whirring noise coming from the floor, and Kedrick was very worried indeed about what might be happening. Then, the crucible began to light up, and light poured out of it into the air, like some kind of rainbow. The rainbow started to flicker faster, and faster and then form images in front of Kedrick and to either side of him, three images in total. He heard the story of the images as they played faster and faster; he couldn't even see the images to his sides, but somehow, he knew what they were showing him. The images put Kedrick into a trance-like state, and information flowed into him like water over a riverbed, totally submersing his consciousness for several hours until finally, the crucible suddenly went dark, and the medallion was released and fell to the floor.

Kedrick stood motionless, his gaze fixed on an imaginary world that existed only in his mind. The bustling reality around him faded into the background as he became lost in his thoughts. Time slipped away unnoticed; he remained in a trance-like state for another fifteen minutes, completely absorbed in the vivid landscapes and scenarios he envisioned. Slowly, he began to come to his senses, the sounds and sights of the real world gradually breaking through the haze of his imagination. As he blinked and refocused, he was left with a lingering sense of wonder about what he had just experienced.

Gone now was his trance, but he still felt different; he felt that, before, he had walked about with his eyes closed to the world around him, but now he knew about everything, about things long forgotten and things never known. He knew that Ellowed was indeed his ancestor, and that a crown awaited his taking in Graigeth, as the rightful heir, which concerned him less. He knew Ellowed had made a mess of Graigeth because, after building Targon, Ellowed had tried to make a city in the snow using his knowledge of industry to heat it, but instead of making a wonderful city like Targon, he had got it wrong and polluted the land in the process, a pollution that still continued to this day. After Ellowed realised his mistakes, he sought help from the Cave of Visions, but the information was too great for him, in his declining years, to grasp. His mind was no longer as open, and that is when he found out about the prophecy! Most importantly, Kedrick now knew how to put right the problems. The prophecy would come true!

# Enter The King

Graigeth was not far from the Cave of Visions, only half a day's journey. The main trouble for Kedrick would be getting past one of two garrison posts. You see, the routes into the city passed by one or the other, whichever way he chose to take. He figured the nearest post would be the safest, as the cave had suggested there was nothing of importance to Graigeth to guard here, since they did not know about the Cave of Visions, and the other garrison post was near the mines of the city which was held very dear indeed, and therefore, would not be well guarded at all. Hopefully, the men from the posts had been recalled to join the army of Graigeth, which would allow Kedrick to pass freely through the mountain pass to the city where he needed to go. At least, that was his thought, guessing that it probably wouldn't be that easy.

After being in a trance for so long, Kedrick stepped out of the cave and realised it was morning. The sky had a red glow, as if it were on fire; it was stunning, and in just half an hour, it would fade away, replaced by the harsh, common light of day. The snowstorm had also lifted, leaving the mountains looking fresh and rejuvenated. From his high vantage point, everything appeared bright and alive. Kedrick wondered if he was simply seeing the world differently now.

Descending the mountain was easy, and halfway down, Kedrick spotted the garrison post. It looked empty, but he still took his time and carefully crept past the post, keeping as far away from it as he could, just in case it was inhabited. The bad news for Kedrick was that the post was inhabited, but its occupants had left on a hunting expedition an hour ago and were just returning with their catch of wild boar! Unfortunately, as Kedrick was looking at the post and carefully sneaking past, he walked right into the enemy, who wasted no time in restraining him and taking him back to their post. "What do you think you are doing here in the mountains of our King Driscol?" Asked the Guardsman, "I am the true heir to the throne of Graigeth, here is my seal of royalty!", stated Kedrick as he handed the medallion over to the guard! "Oh, beg my pardon, your highness!" Jested the guard, as his colleague snatched the rucksack off Kedrick's back. The first guard held the medallion up to his colleague, "This will be worth a few drinks at the tavern!" he said, smiling. "Here, take a look at this", said the other guard, holding the feathers wrapped in leaves. "What do you think he has hidden here?", "It's probably worth money, be more careful, you'll drop it! Bring it here.", said the first guard, getting involved in the unwrapping of the leaves on the counter. "No, don't open that!" cried Kedrick. "See, I told you it was worth something, he doesn't want us to see it!" said the first guard. As they both unwrapped the leaves their faces changed from excitement to bewilderment as they saw the feathers, "What is this?", asked the second guard as they both picked up the feathers and quickly dropped them again, "What is goin....", is all the first guard could say before the paralysis took over and the two men fell to the floor unable to control their legs. "These are feathers from a Giant Crascus, and I am the true king of Graigeth! Now I must be on my way, goodbye!" he said, and Kedrick gathered his gear, again carefully wrapping the feathers in the leaves and placing them at the bottom of his bag.

Following a path down the rest of the mountainside, it wasn't long before Kedrick was just outside the walls of the city. He didn't actually know what to do next, so he left the path and disappeared into the bushes and trees, and waited and watched the goings-on of the city. He thought that knowing what was happening would give him an idea of what to do next! He didn't even know what to say to the people of Graigeth; it just hadn't crossed his mind, and he didn't even know if they spoke the same language as him.

After an hour, Kedrick was formulating a plan. He would have to make a grand entrance into the city. Something that would capture everyone's imagination, enough to gather support as the rightful heir to the throne. Maybe he could make a vehicle that would float out of the crael? It could be done, but it would take time. As he didn't have a better plan, he guessed any plan is better than no plan at all and started looking around for branches he could bind together. There were plenty of fallen branches and vines about the place, so he got to work in a clearing out of sight of the path and started to put his vehicle together. With his new understanding of engineering, he found designing a vehicle easy work and had put the main bones of the vehicle together with the help of his sword within an hour, and had completed the whole vehicle, bar the propulsion baskets, after three hours of diligent work. However, the propulsion baskets, of which five were needed, took two more hours alone as they had to be perfect to do the job. Each basket had five closed sides and one open side; the closed sides held degrelite stones to shield the effects of the crael, to focus the effect purely on the open side. The crael, of course, was held in place behind a partition of branches. The only thing he was missing was the source of its power, the crael itself. At the moment, all his entire floating vehicle would do was lie on the ground, but Kedrick knew how to get his magical fuel. He would have to wait until nightfall.

As darkness fell, Kedrick pulled his cloak far over his head and took the five traps he had made into the city of Graigeth. It was dark, and no one noticed him walking the streets. As he neared the crael plant, he could have sworn he heard Asthal and Captain Blades' voices, but when he looked, all he could see were creatures. He climbed the outside stairs of the chimney to the very top, making sure he didn't step on anyone along the way. Once at the top, completely unnoticed, he held the first trap open over the chimney and waited. Just as he had suspected, not long after, a lump of crael flew up and out of the chimney and into Kedrick's trap. The force of the crael hitting the trap Kedrick was holding nearly enough to throw him from the chimney altogether, but he managed to stay where he was and closed the trap, locking the crael inside and deflecting its power. A further four times, he held out a trap until, eventually, he was done and made his way slowly back down the highly occupied chimney. As he was passing a Tavern, a creature was thrown out to the floor right in front of him, and he quickly stepped back into the shadows, so as not to be discovered. Two more creatures came out of the Tavern, and the first kicked the creature lying on the ground in the leg, "Get up and fight!" said the first creature, kicking him again. Slowly the creature on the floor got to his feet, "You can't beat me!", he said, in a drunken voice, raising his hands ready to box, "I am going to kick you as…", his words left him as he took a punch to the chin from the first creature and fell flat on his back! He had been knocked out. The other two creatures laughed and went back into the Tavern to have a drink. Kedrick came out of the shadows and paused for only a second, looking at the face of the creature. It looked very much like Jim Dobb, which made Kedrick think, 'We are the same!' For years, ever since Kedrick had been a boy,

Kevlarian's had looked down upon the people of the city, calling them creatures or wild animals, but now, looking upon this drunken fool's face, he could see that it was wrong; the only difference between a Kevlarian and a person from this city was the hair growth seen on the Graigeth person.

Aware of the task ahead, Kedrick snapped himself out of his philosophising and once again crept off down the dark streets of Graigeth.

Back at the vehicle, he carefully moved the crael from his traps to the correct places and fastened them securely in place. It was done. In front of him, his vehicle floated. He climbed aboard, and it held his weight soundly. He manoeuvred a little, and it responded perfectly like the miracle of engineering that it was. Kedrick had used local stones to line his crael baskets, as the local stones are high in degrelite.

In the morning, he would make his entrance as the new King! But for now, Kedrick used a vine to lash his vehicle to a tree. Using the two lumps of crael he planned on using for steering his vehicle, he put them together in a wooden cage he had made, and the warmth they gave out from being together and reacting with each other kept him warm throughout the night, as he had hoped they would. In fact, they kept him so warm that he slept too long and missed all the commotion of the army going into battle and woke to find the city unusually quiet.

After some contemplation as to whether he should wait for a bigger audience to appear, Kedrick noticed the sound of cattle, and that sound did not fit in with a city, unless.... unless today was market day, in which case everyone would be at the market! Could this get any better, he thought? Without further thought, Kedrick fixed in place his two steering baskets and mounted his vehicle. Today will be remembered in history, he thought, as he untethered the vehicle and turned the steering baskets around to guide him out of the bushes and onto the path. Kedrick's luck was in as he drove through the rear gates to the city unchallenged, as all guards had been posted to the front wall of the city. Kedrick followed the sound of the cattle and the shouting of voices that matched the market sounds of Thurk!

Gently hovering above the streets, three feet off the ground, in perfect control, Kedrick moved his craft slowly down the narrow streets of Graigeth towards the raucous of the market. A few people did stop and stare at the phenomenal machine and the gleaming knight in armour as they passed, and everyone got well out of its way. As Kedrick neared the crowd at the marketplace, the loud shouting suddenly stopped as everyone turned to look. Even the cattle seemed to be intrigued by this strange vehicle as they too fell silent. Kedrick steered his vehicle into the middle of the crowd and put it into park. He looked around at all the hairy faces watching him and for a second, he felt quite nervous, but then he said in a loud voice, "Here is the Royal Seal of Ellowed", holding up his medallion, "I am Kedrick Ellowed. Rightful King of Graigeth!" He waited for a response, but everyone remained silent! Was it an attentive audience hanging on his every word, or would they attack him? Kedrick prayed it was the first scenario and went on, "Accept me as your King and I will provide clean, safe heat to you all and you will have clean air to breathe, instead of this filth you have today!" The crowd started chatting among themselves. Kedrick could not make out a single word that was being said by his audience and still feared that they would attack him. The chattering went on for nearly a minute, then one solitary man bowed and spoke, "I am your servant, your majesty". This began a chain reaction in the crown, and soon everyone had sworn allegiance to Kedrick.

Just then, as things were looking up, King Driscol, who had been notified of events in the marketplace, turned up. "What pray is going on here?" Looking Kedrick up and down, he said," Guards, arrest this man!" Kedrick knew he couldn't let the guards arrest him, as all would be lost, so he raised his sword and pointed it at them, "Dare you arrest me! Kedrick Ellowed, true and rightful king of Graigeth!" he said. The Guards looked betwixt, not knowing what to do, "Arrest him, I say, it is trickery, I am your king!" argued Driscol.

Nervous shouts came from the crowd who had lived in fear of Driscol's harsh rule for many years, "Kill the stranger!", "Hang him!", "He's a Liar!".

Kedrick decided to repeat his offer, "Accept me as the rightful king of Graigeth, and I will provide you with clean heat and clean air to breathe instead of the dirty smog there is today!"

A deafening silence fell upon the crowd, and the guards looked at Kedrick and stepped forward toward him. Then they stopped and looked at the crowd. The crowd was whispering now, "He might be the King, he has powers!" "He might be the King!" After a moment, both guards kneeled in front of Kedrick. "Hail King Ellowed," they said, bowing their heads.

Driscol knew he had lost the battle for his kingdom and the only way to regain it would be to kill Kedrick, so, without warning, he let loose his sword and lunged towards Kedrick, who instinctively raised his own sword and defended the strike by pushing Driscol's sword to the left sending the ex-king stumbling into a pile of wooden barrels. "Guards seize him and lock him up!" Kedrick demanded, and the guards turned and approached Driscol. They picked him up from the barrels, and surprisingly, Driscol didn't fight them. But once he was on his feet, he freed one of the guard's swords from its scabbard and pushed the other over a barrel, and the fight for kingship was back on again! This time, his first parry and strike took Kedrick by surprise; it landed on his right arm, cutting deeply just below his shoulder. Stunned and in pain, Kedrick stumbled backwards, barely getting his sword raised sufficiently to deflect Driscol's second blow. Kedrick quickly swapped hands and stance and dodged Driscol's next attack. He parried forward at Driscol, but his attack was easily deflected as he had never practised swordsmanship with his left hand, and everything now felt backwards and clumsy! Driscol laughed as he landed another swipe of his sword, this time to Kedrick's right thigh, as he had left himself open to attack. The pain seared, and his vision blurred as Kedrick stumbled back, trying to get away from Driscol before he attacked again. Then the pain coming from his left arm told him that he was fast enough, as Driscol had successfully landed another sword swipe. Now holding his sword with both hands, Kedrick was just about managing to avoid further injury as his senses recovered enough to keep himself alive. Driscol was good with his sword, but predictively, though, he would try and land a strike to the right, and then to one to the left and so on. Kedrick was deflecting each attack, but taking a step back each time, too, and behind him lay a wall about five steps back! If he let Driscol beat him back against the wall, he would be done for, and he knew it! But Driscol was driven, and there was no sign of him tiring as Kedrick deflected strike after strike again, and again. Kedrick felt cold as his clothes soaked up the blood from his wounds, and the blurred vision was trying to creep in again as he deflected yet another strike! Then, as the power of the strike pushed him half over to the right, he saw a cobble missing in the ground to the right and put all his remaining energy into lurching himself to the right over and past the missing cobble! His play paid off as Driscol's attention was fully focused on destroying Kedrick, and he didn't see the missing cobble and stumbled on the pothole, allowing Kedrick to land a double-handed strike down upon him, which was met by Driscol's sword. Kedrick knew it was do-or-die time; soon, he would have no energy to hold his sword. He brought his sword down again, and again on Driscol. Both attacks were met by Driscol's sword, but at least Kedrick was the one attacking now!

On Kedrick's next attack, Driscol had recovered, and his deflection sent Kedrick stumbling to the left into the wall! Face in the wall, Kedrick somehow felt Driscol raise his sword, ready to bring it down on Kedrick. He sensed the sky-high raised sword being released into a downfall and side-stepped the attack, and Driscol's sword clanged into the solid wall, where Kedrick had been. Kedrick swung around quickly and brought his sword down upon Driscol's, snapping the blade in half! He then held his sword to Driscol's neck. Disarmed, Driscol was beaten, and Kedrick ordered the guards to apprehend him.

The crowd, eagerly watching the fight and secretly hoping for Kedrick to win, fell to their knees, acknowledging him as their new ruler. Just then, a voice called from the city's main gates, "The enemy is

attacking! Man the walls!" "What enemy?" Kedrick
shouted, "Hold your fire, hold your fire!" he repeated as
he made his way to the main gates, guided by men
running in the same direction. As he reached the gate,
he found there was no room to climb the stairs for the
many bodies in the way, "Let me through, I am your
king!" He only needed to speak once, and the men
immediately parted to let the King through. As Kedrick
reached the top of the battlements above the gate, he
breathed a sigh of relief. He would not have to defend
his new kingdom tonight! Walking towards the gate was
the Army of Targon, with Asthal near the front line.
"It is okay; they are our allies. Open the gate!" shouted
Kedrick, running down to meet the friendly faces he
now felt he knew so well. As the Army approached the
elaborate metal gates, they opened with a loud cranking
noise coming from the gatehouses on either side of the
entrance, and Kedrick stepped forward to greet the new
allies of Graigeth.

   "Are you the king of this land?" demanded the
General in charge, before Asthal could reach him to
brief him about Kedrick. "Indeed, I am, sir, I am the
new king of Graigeth and seeing that you ride under
Queen Dubark's colours and with my good friend
Asthal, I would like to invite you and your men into our
city under the flag of peace and friendship!"
By this time, Asthal had reached the General: "This is
Kedrick. He was sent here on a mission by Queen

Dubark, and he is our ally. "Very well, your majesty, we kindly accept your invitation. Please lead on!"

With that, Kedrick turned and walked back to his vehicle, this time with a hundred horseshoes clattering on the cobbles behind him. When he reached his own floating craft, the eyes of the allies behind him nearly popped out of their sockets, for they too had never heard about or seen such a vehicle before. Kedrick asked one of the royal guards who had betrayed Driscol earlier in favour of a fairer king to show him to the royal Palace, and the guard happily led on. Kedrick followed. The Palace looked elaborate, but being so dark and sooty did not suit it. The interior was clean and beautifully decorated, much like the Palace at Targon. "Show me to the diplomatic chamber, please", demanded Kedrick politely. As they walked, Asthal walked beside Kedrick, "Do you realise that you can speak Graigeth?", "What do you mean, I can't?" "You clearly made it to the Cave of Visions, Kedrick. You display knowledge that you did not have before, and when you spoke to the guard before, you spoke in Graigeth!" "Really, but I just spoke the same as I always do?", "No, you didn't, you must be adjusting your language on a subconscious basis".

As they entered the room, Kedrick turned to the guard, "Could you please arrange for all my leaders and chiefs to join me? We have a lot to discuss together", Kedrick said, closing the big door.

"You did it, young Kedrick! You completed your treacherous quest, I knew you would!", "I nearly didn't, Asthal! On a number of occasions, I nearly strayed from the path! "I have to admit, Kedrick, I did intervene a couple of times when I felt a tremor in the paths of flow, telling me that your quest was in serious trouble! I sent a light to guide your footsteps in the right direction. "I remember seeing a light near the Cave of Visions, in the fog when I couldn't see, it was so bright, it drew me toward it! "Yes, I feared that had you not followed my light, you would have plummeted from the eastern cliff of the mountain!"

It is rather important to remember at this point that the ancient folklore of Mantle, that is, the really deep folklore that only Asthal and his apprentice know about, states that not only was the whole of Mantle joined by invisible interlocking paths that allowed pure energy to flow and ebb around Mantle, but that the old stories indicated the flow of energy originated from the creation of Mantle by the Gods. And by building and walking upon the invisible paths, the flow could be harnessed. Which is why the clever Asthal saw that his house was quite deliberately rebuilt where five paths of flow crossed, to increase his magical powers. It is said that when the old Gods created Mantle, the excess energy was so strong that many ordinary, uneducated folks developed magical powers, causing the creation of many wizarding families, who, in turn, in the quest for even greater powers, took the land of Mantle into a very dark place. They battled fiercely against one another, using and wasting larger and larger amounts of raw magic in their pointless incantations. This continued until they had drained all but every drop of magic in Mantle.

Then one by one, the inheritance of magical powers simply did not get passed on. Which, of course, saw fewer and fewer wizards, and that is how it went up to the present day, when just Asthal remained. No one knew where the magic had gone, for it is also said that the energy that flowed could never vanish; it could be used, but in using it, it would simply be transported or transmuted for a period of time before it would revert to its original form and therefore, ultimately never diminish the overall flow. But for some reason, the flow did diminish, and no one really knew why.

Asthal had suspicions about where the energy had gone, but they were just that, and he had been investigating to see if he was right. The wizard had only managed to possess his own magical powers through the educated manner that saw him develop them. For he was not born a wizard, nor was he from one of the wizarding families of old, as you may have thought! No, his father had been a sparring partner for battle training for the royal family. And, as such, he had lived in the palace with his family, and that is where young Asthal caught the eye of the resident scholar who taught the children of the royal house. He gained many hours of personal tutoring, giving him the gift of reading and setting him on a path of discovery. He learned about the magic of old, read about the paths of energy, and developed expertise in old methods of conjuring using the energy. In time, he found books with old spells in and developed more into the wizard he is today. Now, he was teaching this knowledge to his apprentice, not only the skill of acquiring knowledge, but also about using that knowledge with responsibility, unlike the wizards of old! Education was his primary interest, and he knew Kedrick would, having visited the Cave of Visions, have some knowledge that may clarify matters for him.

"Drink this potion, Kedrick! Fore, it will heal your wounds," said the wizard as he handed Kedrick a small, purple-coloured vial of liquid. Asthal was keenly interested in the ability of Kedrick's floating transport and what knowledge had led him to build the transport! "How did you come about the floating transport that you have?" "It seemed to be a good idea at the time to grab the attention of the people of Graigeth! The Cave of Visions showed me how close Ellowed had come to creating the perfect city here, high in the mountains, but he made one mistake, which has led to the poisoning of our lakes, rivers and lands! The plants here burn a rock mined from the mountains called crael. Contained in the rock is an energy source that can be harnessed for use in so many ways. It can generate heat with no fire, and it can make things float, as well as so much more. To make the transport float, I had to line cages on all but one side with dragolite, which exists naturally in the mountains and shields the effect of the crael rock.", "I knew it!" expressed Asthal, "The energy of old that caused magic to flow strongly across Mantle has been trapped and stored by this dragolite in the mountains! It all makes perfect sense! Well done, Kedrick, you really have done an excellent job!"

Then a knock at the door saw King Kedrick's official advisors and political members of council enter, announced by the royal guard of Graigeth, "Melthwy, Councillor of Warmth, Ogwyn, Councillor of War and Gomer Ashbull from the City Planners' office" Kedrick had obviously made a big impression on the people of Graigeth with his entrance and the ousting of Driscol as King! The men entered rather sheepishly. While councillors normally need assistance in keeping quiet, these two looked as though they would need help in talking! "Thank you all for coming at such short notice! I expect a change of King will be hard enough for you to get used to, but I also have very important changes to make in how things are run here, but don't worry, the changes are for the better of Graigeth and will also benefit the whole of Mantle." "Firstly, Melthwy and Gomer, you need to make significant changes to the generation of heat in this city! You must know about the effect the plants are having on Graigeth. I have been here but one day, and nearly everyone that I have met has a bad cough!"

"We are aware that adjustments are needed, and we have been working on different filters for the chimney made from Cockspur grass and nettle juice. There has been some success!", Melthwy put out in tender as an answer. "Some success?" inquired King Kedrick. "Yes, the filter worked a bit, but then it was destroyed as a lump of crael hit it and caused it to collapse into the chimney and burn away!" "I see; well, I have to say that I have a solution that will avoid the need for filters, is easy to manufacture, and has been within your grasp all this time!" Kedrick could see that his words had caught the imagination of the councillors, who had no doubt spent too many years sitting in their cold living rooms, coughing due to the bad air quality here. Their eyes glistened just as a child's eyes would if a dessert were produced for them after dinner. "We will stop burning crael in the plants soon, but to start with, can I ask you how good the carpenters of Graigeth are at building wooden cages?" "Our carpenters are among the best; we have a building where they spend long hours learning the craft and developing their skills!" answered the councillors. "Good. We need wooden cages built to my exact instructions, one cage per family. We will then use two lumps of crael in each cage, and by adjusting the distance the crael is from each other, the cage will warm the family's house without any harmful smoke." "That sounds good, but won't the wooden cage catch fire?" "No, we will set a minimum distance between the two lumps of crael to prevent it from getting too hot, but we will work out the details later with a bit of trial and error"

King Kedrick turned to Ogwyn "The army of Graigeth surrendered today to the army of Targon!" "I can only humbly apologise for our failings in battle, Your Majesty!", added Ogwyn in hurried apology.
"I know that is a bitter pill for you to swallow, but the truth of the matter is that Graigeth is now allied with Targon. I don't see that any man failed in their duty today. Ultimately, responsibility lies with Driscol, who sent out the army of Graigeth only half prepared for the battle!" "Targon's army is well-trained and disciplined, and I would like our army to undergo extra training at Targon! If, as you say, we have the best carpentry training scheme on the whole of Mantle, then I feel I can come to some kind of arrangement with the Queen to open our carpentry scheme to the carpenters of Targon in return for military skill training." "Well, I feel our men are highly trained already, but since the army of Targon did indeed gain the upper hand in battle over them, I will back your suggestion of an exchange training scheme with the Army of Targon." "Good, then that is decided." "Now, Melthwy, come here and I will draw a design for the heater box", and both men stepped towards the table.

In conclusion of the first introductions, Chef Kinio, who was the head chef at the palace, met with King Kedrick the First. Chef Kinio was as jolly as he was round, and a pleasure to speak with, unlike some of the tight-lipped political leaders with whom he had spent much of his time this day. Chef Kinio was very happy to hear the news of the open borders, as there was so little growing within the city, to allow him to prepare the dishes of excellence that he had so wanted to make. He suggested that a big feast be held in a week's time to celebrate the official crowning of Kedrick and the start of a new era in the history books of Graigeth, to which Kedrick agreed.

As the evening drew to a close, Kedrick and his recently found friends from Targon left the official chambers. Each was led by a guide to their personal quarters. Kedrick could hear the Chef cheerfully shouting orders to his staff, already preparing for the feast.

Kedrick was amazed at how similar the architecture was between the Palaces of Targon and of Graigeth. He had to again tell himself that they would be similar, as the same man, Ellowed, designed both Palaces!

His guide led him into the royal quarters, and Kedrick's jaw dropped as he took in the splendour of the room. The opulent décor, featuring gold and silver brocade on a crimson ground, served as a backdrop for paintings depicting historical events by artists unknown to him. The rich textures of the fabrics felt luxurious under his fingertips, inviting him to explore every inch. The air was thick with the scent of polished wood and fresh flowers, mingling with a hint of beeswax from the flickering candles that cast a warm glow throughout the chamber. No matter where he looked, something captured his full attention; there was too much to absorb all at once. The attention to detail in every aspect of the room was incredibly inspiring, clearly indicating that the finest craftsmen in the land had been employed. The coolness of the marble floor contrasted with the warmth of the richly embroidered tapestries swaying gently in the draft. Although Kedrick wished to sit and study every last detail, he was too tired; it had been a long and eventful day. He had gone from being a farmhand to a miller's apprentice, and now he had transitioned from being a knight to becoming a king! The weight of the crown seemed to linger in his mind, both exhilarating and exhausting. It was definitely time to sleep.

As the new king slept, his mind wasn't truly at rest; it was turning over and over the same old story. He would see Flankell the Gelf, whom he had met and left behind on the Plains of Confusion. The Gelf was really ill; he could momentarily see the world through the eyes of the Gelf, the horizon was just spinning around, and then he fell to the floor, roughly, banging his head hard on the dusty, dry earth of the plain. Then it would start all over again, and so on. When Kedrick finally awoke, he was weary, tired from his bad dreams and filled with a strong sense of foreboding for Flankell. He was a man driven by his concerns, and if his feelings were right, he had to act now to try and save Flankell! "Load my vehicle with a hamper of food and drink", he shouted to his butler, Gerard, as he left his chambers still in the midst of fastening his shirt. "And have my vehicle brought to the front entrance, is Asthal about? Where can I find him?" his servants led him to the wise wizard, who was eating breakfast alone in a corner of the main dining room. As always, he had a calm persona and greeted the new king's fraught expression with the same all-knowing and nothing-bothering look that inhabited his face so well. And in fairness, the old wizard was just about the most intelligent person living on Mantle at that precise moment in time. "I need your counsel, Asthal. My dreams disturb my soul; they show a Gelf I met called Flankell, who appears to be dying! "Do they tell me the truth, for I can feel this fate is impending in my bones! Am I just suffering from a night of poor sleep?". The wizard put the slice of Loaf that he had been eating down onto his plate and looked at Kedrick. His eyebrows moved a little closer as if he was trying to decide the best way to describe something complicated, to someone very simple! "The fate of your friend is indeed in question. I can sense that the Yama is very close to him! If you take no action, he may pass into the other realm." "Then I must take my leave and make my best efforts to uphold a promise I made to his wife and son. Thank you for your counsel", and with that, King Kedrick made his exit to where his prepared vehicle was waiting for him, only it did look a little different. Gone were the roughly twined together reeds that had been used; gone were the tree branches, and instead floated a highly crafted vehicle that had comfortable seating for four people, which was truly worthy of a king. The craft floated a whole foot higher in the air, too, which surprised Kedrick as he thought that with all the fineries, he could see that it would be heavier, not lighter. "Please forgive us, your Majesty, but we took the initiative to refine your basic design and put our best craftsmen to work after you arrived yesterday on re-crafting your vehicle, the newer design proved lighter due to the wood they used so I am sorry it rides higher, they have built in fold down steps to get in though. I had hoped it would be painted before you required using it, but it is fully functional.", "There is no need to apologise, the craftsmen have done a beautiful job, it is indeed a fine craft now! I must leave on urgent business, but assure everyone that I will return in time for the official crowning and the feast!"

With that, he set off in his new craft, which was far better than he had imagined it could be. Being lighter, it moved faster too and responded far better with its better constructed design. He soared across the countryside like a bird gliding on a breath of wind. He followed the winding way of the open valleys as much as he could, for he had to take care of through the forest, for avoiding smacking into trees was very difficult when travelling at high speed. Zooming across the valley floors, Kedrick scared quite a few deer, who had never seen anything like his vehicle before, and then scattered away into the safety of the forest.

As lunchtime neared, he had the River Qualm in sight and the food the chef had thrust at him as he left the palace, but he knew there was not a moment to waste. Every second he delayed his journey would be a second closer to death for Flankell! With this in mind, he pushed his craft harder, and within five minutes of crossing the river, he reached Flankell. Just as he slowed his craft down, the vision he had seen over and over came true. Flankell fell to the floor right in front of him. Kedrick jumped down from the craft in haste and scooped the thin, tiny little Gelf up and placed him across the rear seats of the craft. The crafts rebuild had seen the rear seats given much more in the way of passenger protection, with higher sides to reduce the chance of anyone falling out during transit. Making them perfect for the unconscious Flankell. He checked his vital signs and reassured himself that Flankell was still alive. Then, gently, he tried to get some fresh water past his lips, making Flankell choke as his body desperately tried to accept the gift. He knew Flankell would not fall out if he came to a bit more and started moving about. So, after helping Flankell take a little water, he hurriedly sped off on his way towards the far end of the plains with a view to taking Flankell to his family at the hidden Gelf village.

After ten minutes, the craft was shifting at a speed that kicked up dust from the dry ground as he sped over it! He was pushing it as hard as he could, taking it to its limit and then beyond. The whole craft shook and vibrated but held together thanks to the incredible carpentry skills of the Graigeth carpenters. The shaking disturbed Flankell from his unconsciousness, "My wife, she is with me!" he said, totally delirious, "Yes, she is alive, I have met her", said Kedrick, "I am taking you to her, you will be together again soon, Flankell". A brief smile flashed over Flankell's face as the words Kedrick had uttered partially struck some part of his mind, but then the smile left as he fell unconscious again! Knowing he had to hurry if he wanted Flankell to survive, he turned his drive systems to the full speed ahead configuration, for he had found that his craft continually increased its speed, and very soon he was travelling so fast that the wind pressed in hard against his face as the craft flew over the ground. A growl started to be emitted from the vehicle's baskets, and the shaking and vibrating grew so vigorous that it felt as though the craft could flip over out of control at any moment. Hence, he momentarily adjusted the drive systems to the parked configuration, and the craft slowed a little, and the growl disappeared. Kedrick was now the fastest person on Mantle! Soon, he had cleared the plains and changed his speed to a crawl as he carefully steered his craft up the edge of the volcanic crater to the opening. He parked his craft there and carried Flankell the rest of the way down into the crater's heart. As he came into sight, screams of disbelief filled the air, and a group of Gevlings took the burden of Flankell's frail body away from Kedrick, taking him away to what must have been his family's hut. The fever of excitement did not end there as the medicine man came running past Kedrick to the hut where Flankell was. All the commotion suddenly ceased, the screaming of the women, the shouting of the men, even the excited playful noises of the Gelf children all stopped, as everyone waited with bated breath to see the outcome of the medicine man's visit.

The fate of Flankell hung in the balance, half passed on into the next world, and only his love for his son and wife faintly anchored him to this one. No one dared to guess what the outcome would be. In most cultures, the medicine men used displays of trickery to make it look as if they had magic powers, but not here, for the medicine men of the Gelf were truly magical. They knew magic as old as the mountains, if not older, but rarely used it, keeping their powers out of sight, but ready to intervene in a heartbeat in any emergency. Flankell was in good hands; he had the best chance of surviving now that the medicine man was with him. Minutes passed, and no one came out of the hut. Minutes turned into a quarter of an hour, then half an hour, then an hour later, the medicine man left the hut with a smile on his face, and everyone knew Flankell was going to be fine. Kedrick had changed his fate with his speedy rescue. Everything seemed to have finally fallen into place! He knew his ancestry, he had stopped the rot, and the land was recovering; two kingdoms were finally coming together. It couldn't get any better than this, Kedrick thought. He also wondered what new quests lay ahead of him, what new missions would he have to lead as King!

# THE FEAST

The day of the grand banquet finally dawned, and the great hall of the palace, once a silent and foreboding place, now hummed with the joyous chaos of a thousand voices. The very air, thick with the scent of roasted venison, spiced apple cider, and the sweet earthiness of baked yams, felt alive with a palpable sense of triumph. Golden torchlight danced on the high, carved ceilings, casting moving shadows on the faces of lords and common folk alike, their shared exhaustion from the war replaced by an almost giddy relief.

Below, the city of Graigeth shimmered under a clear night sky. For the first time in generations, the stars were not a faint, smudged memory but a brilliant, countless spattering of silver light against the dark canvas above, a silent testament to the efforts of the new king to remove the chimneys that had belched out a sooty poison before.

Kedrick, now king, felt the immense new weight of his crown as a heavy presence on his brow. Being responsible for more than his own well-being was much harder than questing through his many trials.

The feasting hall was an endless, churning sea of jubilant faces, each one looking to him, their new monarch, for a word, a smile, a sign of hope. He moved through the crowd, a tireless automaton, his face set in a practised mask of dignified joy, his hand extended to be clasped by countless others. He heard their blessings and their thanks, their stories of hardship and deliverance, each one a warm, sincere gesture, but the sheer volume of it all was overwhelming. Every smile, every handshake, every moment of conversation was a new duty, a new expectation. He was no longer just Kedrick, the weary hero; he was King Kedrick, a symbol, and the persona felt like a beautiful, suffocating mask.

This profound, bone-deep fatigue drove him to find a small, shadowed archway, and, with a subtle nod to a nearby guard, he slipped away from the radiant clamour of the feast.

A wave of relief washed over him as he emerged onto a stone balcony. The air here was cool and thin, a stark contrast to the stifling warmth of the hall. He stood for a moment, the sounds of the celebration, footsteps echoing against the marble floors, a distant roar behind him. He simply took it all in: the cool kiss of the night wind, the hushed murmur of the ancient palace, the vast, shimmering expanse of the stars above.

It was then he saw her, the Princess, standing alone in a small, serene garden below, her back to him as she gazed at the heavens. Her dress, the colour of a winter sky, was a soft, elegant contrast to the chaos of the feast, its fabric whispering as the night breeze caught it.

He descended the stairs, his boots making no sound on the mossy path. "Your Highness," he began, his voice a little softer than he had intended.

She turned, her eyes, the colour of a deep forest, meeting his. A smile, slow and genuine, touched her lips. "I just needed to get away from the madness of it all for a few moments of quiet reflection. There are so many people." He nodded, a deep understanding passing between them, "I know, it's .. overwhelming."

They stood in comfortable silence for a long moment, the sounds of the celebration a warm, distant hum, broken only by the chirping of unseen crickets. The moonlight cast them in an ethereal glow. Two people, one a newly crowned king, the other a freed Princess, finally met not as symbols but as simple human beings who shared a common, overwhelming burden.

A commotion in the hall drew Kedrick's attention. A man, dressed in finery so opulent it stood out even in the lavish setting, was dancing with a woman of high public standing named Louisa. He was a picture of effortless charm, his dark eyes sparkling as he spun his partner with an easy grace. Kedrick had spoken to him earlier, finding him to be a most pleasant and honourable man, a seasoned captain of some merchant vessel.

The music suddenly cut out with a jarring screech. A portly official, his face a mottled crimson with rage and wine, pointed a trembling finger at the dancing captain. It was Louisa's own father, the Lord Chamberlain, who shrieked, his voice echoing in the shocked silence. "There he is! The scoundrel! He is no captain of honour, but Captain Rock! The Pirate!" A group of the Chamberlain's private guards pushed forward, their hands on their swords. Louisa froze, her face a mask of dawning horror and betrayal, her gaze locked on her father.

Captain Rock, however, did not flinch. He faced the three guards who had drawn their swords, looking calm but dangerously amused. When the first guard lunged, he didn't counter with a vicious thrust. Instead, his rapier, a whisper of steel, parried the blow and, with a precise twist of his wrist, sent the guard's sword clattering to the marble floor. The second guard moved in, a clumsy, powerful swing aimed at his head. Captain Rock ducked under the blow, his movements impossibly fluid, and spun his blade, deflecting the guard's weapon out of his hand and sending it also skittering across the floor. He sidestepped the third guard's attack, a clean, elegant sidestep that put him behind the man, before a final, practised flick of his wrist disarmed him too.

He was a whirlwind of controlled chaos, a master swordsman who had no intention of drawing blood. He simply smiled, a flash of genuine, reckless amusement on his face. He bowed to Louisa, who stood motionless, her father's furious words still hanging in the air. "Farewell, my lady," he said, his voice a low fond murmur that was meant for her ears alone. With a final, lingering look of profound regret and devotion, he turned and, with an astonishing leap, vaulted a banquet table, disappearing into the crowd and through an open side door, leaving the hall in stunned silence.

The music had not yet resumed. In the sudden quiet, a few whispered shouts followed the pirate's escape. Kedrick watched the guards scurry about, retrieving their fallen swords, their faces a mixture of frustration and disbelief. It had been an invigorating display of skill, a worldly challenge of wits and steel. Yet, his gaze lingered on the open doorway. He had always been a good judge of character, and his gut told him the man was not a villain. The effortless way he had disarmed the guards without a single intention of harm, that was not the action of a ruthless man. He was sure, with a deep certainty, that whatever he had done to earn the title of "pirate" must have been a deeply misunderstood act of goodness. He knew right then, that if their paths ever crossed again, he would do his best to get to the bottom of the matter, and if he was right, he would be the one to pardon him.

On the other side of the room, Louisa stood, her face pale, her hands clasped tightly together as she stared at the empty doorway. She did not look like a woman who had just had a brush with a scoundrel, but rather a woman who had just lost something precious. The guards muttered their frustration, and Kedrick felt a ghostly presence beside him for a brief, silent moment. A wry, almost imperceptible smile touched the spectral lips of his fallen friend, Captain Blade, a shared understanding that this was a world far more complex than they had ever been led to believe. Kedrick nodded to the vanishing image, feeling that some connection existed between his fallen friend and the pirate, "Yes, I will get to the bottom of this matter." He spoke to himself quietly, but also to reassure the captain.

As the night deepened, Asthal found him, his face uncharacteristically grim, his long robes swaying in the wind. "The celebration is a joyous one, my king," he began, his voice a low, resonant murmur, "but I have looked around the palace tonight. There are some here, I believe, who practice a different kind of magic than my own. An ancient magic that I have only ever read about in forgotten old tomes." The wizard's voice lowered to a grim whisper. "I believe they are still loyal to the old king, and I have heard whispers. It is the magic of the dark goblins, and I am positive Driscol brought this evil with him." Asthal's gaze became intensely focused. "Earlier today, I looked around the East Tower, where Driscoll spent considerable time. There is undeniable evidence of this dark magic. He is involved, and he has a following. I suggest extra guards be ordered to the prison to protect against any jailbreak attempts, sire. You must keep your guard up."

The wizard's words were a cold current that ran through the warmth of the celebration, a subtle, but certain, promise of more trials to come. The sword of Targon, hanging at Kedrick's hip, seemed to hum faintly in response, a low thrum that spoke not of rest, but of the long journey ahead. The feast was a celebration of what had been achieved, but it was also a farewell to the old world, a first step into a new, and for many here, uncertain future.

Outside, the air was crisp and invigorating, a stark contrast to the previous days when thick smog hung heavy over the city. A newfound clarity existed within Graigeth's people, their eyes where opening to a new world, in many ways, a better life, but suddenly they had found themselves responsible and accountable for their own actions, rather than merely slaves, institutionalised by the maniacal King Driscol, and Kedrick summised, it was this very accountability that some of his subjects feared, after so many years of simply existing, in a child-like state of being controlled.

In the grand hall, all eyes were on King Kedrick, formerly the humble miller's apprentice, who now sat proudly on his throne. His heart swelled with pride and purpose as he realised the significance of his ascent. He had indeed fulfilled a prophecy of Ellowed, reclaiming the future of these people in a way that would be remembered for generations to come. It felt like a lifetime ago when Captain Blade first recognised the significance of his medallion, a shimmering symbol that had once glinted defiantly against the backdrop of Driscol's tyranny.

The next day, he stood in the main square, his heart heavy with the memory of the valiant captain. Having witnessed his spirit last night, he was comforted to know that he must have seen Mantle's hard-won salvation. The sun cast warm rays across the cobblestones, yet a chill seemed to linger in the air, as if the shadows of the past still whispered their truths.

In the centre of the square loomed a grand statue, the likeness of Captain Blade captured mid-stride, his sword raised boldly as if he were challenging the very sky. Kedrick had painstakingly commissioned this monument; its creation was a celebration of grief and gratitude. Beneath the figure, the names of every brave soul who had fallen were etched into the fresh stone, their legacies preserved for all to see. The final inscription read, "Those who died for a free Graigeth", a powerful reminder of the sacrifice that had paved the way for the nation's new dawn. Yet, amidst the bustling crowds that gathered to pay their respects, murmurs of dissent floated through the air like smoke from a fading fire. A small group of disquieted voices drifted in and out of the celebrations, whispering among themselves with furrowed brows. Some spoke of the former king, Driscol, half human, half goblin, now languishing in a cold prison cell. Their allegiance, although muted, simmered beneath the surface, hinting at an undercurrent of loyalty from those who longed for the days of unchecked power.

Kedrick's gaze darted among the crowd, noticing the dark glint of an eye here, a disapproving scowl there. He could feel the weight of their judgment, an unsettling reminder that not everyone embraced the freedom they had fought so hard to achieve. The laughter of children playing nearby contrasted sharply with the tense whispers, a jarring reminder that while the city celebrated, old wounds still festered in the hearts of some. The warning words of Asthal, the wizard, struck home with the king as he debated in his own mind how he might be able to help settle the fears of his people.

As the sun dipped lower in the sky, casting long shadows that stretched across the square, Kedrick couldn't shake the feeling that not all was well in Graigeth. The people might have put on brave faces, but he sensed the tension that haunted their smiles, the lingering resentment for what had been lost and the fear of what might come next. He wondered if the whispers of dissent would grow louder, if the seeds of discontent might one day sprout into something more ominous. He turned his gaze back to the statue, the resolute figure of Captain Blade, and felt a twinge of determination. If he had to face the shadows of the past, he would do so with all of Graigeth's bravest at his side, ready to defend the fragile peace they had fought so fiercely to secure. But as he moved through the crowd, he couldn't shake the feeling that the winds of change were gathering, howling just beyond the horizon, waiting for the opportune moment to strike.

The nation was experiencing a rebirth of health, at least much healthier than it had been in years. The once-choking smog that hung heavily in the air had dissipated, giving way to crisper, cleaner breezes that carried the scent of blooming wildflowers and freshly turned earth. People could venture outside without the constant scratch in their throats or the tightness in their chests that had plagued them for far too long. The air felt invigorating, filling their lungs with a sense of vitality that had long been missing. However, despite this newfound freshness, remnants of the past still lingered. Many bore the scars of a lifetime spent inhaling toxic fumes; for them, relief was elusive. They coughed occasionally, a guttural reminder of years spent battling unseen foes that left permanent damage in their lungs. The smell of medicinal herbs, blended into potions and salves, floated around the small clinics that had cropped up in neighbourhoods, offering a bittersweet promise of comfort.

The new king, keenly aware of his people's plight, had turned to the legendary wizard for assistance. He requested that Asthal explore any magical remedies that might restore health to those still suffering. It was a desperate plea, tinged with hope, yet the wizard accepted the charge. Not only did he hold extraordinary skill, but he was also a visionary who sensed the rejuvenating magic that had begun to flow through the lands of Mantle once more.

The air buzzed with potential, thick with the hum of energy that crackled like static. Whispers of enchantments filled the corridors of the newly established Academic Veneficus, a school that Asthal, with the complete backing of both King Kedrick and Queen Dubark, created for the education of future wizards. Here, the scent of ancient scrolls and the faint crackle of incantations created a palpable atmosphere of anticipation. Asthal stood proudly as headmaster, unearthing the secrets of magic while guiding eager students. At his side was his apprentice, Grundlenut, who remained a spirited young wizard with an infectious enthusiasm. The aroma of wood smoke and candle wax wafted through the classrooms as they practised spells, their laughter mingling with the soft rustling of pages being turned. The air hummed with the promise of possibility, as the two of them dedicated themselves to exploring the mysteries of magic, and perhaps finding a way to heal those who remained in pain.

Life was noticeably different for everyone, imbued with a sense of anticipation and relief. The Gevlings, once confined to a solitary existence within the old volcanic crater, were finally preparing to leave behind the rugged rock formations and treacherous paths that marked their temporary home. The crater, once a sanctuary from the poisonous miasma that had blanketed the plains, had started to feel more like a cage. Now, the air was clearer, and the vivid colours of the plains beckoned them with promises of life and vitality. As they gathered their belongings, they all could already envision the rolling hills of the plains, dotted with wildflowers and swaying grass. They could almost feel the warm sun on their skin and hear the gentle whispers of the wind as it danced through the tall grasses. Excited murmurs filled the air, mingling with the scents of fresh earth and growing greenery that had recently surfaced after the lifting of the poison.

The Gevlings eagerly set to work, constructing new huts that would be resilient against the elements yet harmonious with the landscape. The familiar sounds of woodworking echoed around them, accompanied by the rhythmic thumps of earth being moved as they prepared their home on the plains. Their laughter mingled with the sounds of nature, slowly restoring the vibrant spirit that had once filled these lands. With each shovel of earth, they planted seeds that held within them the promise of renewal. The rich, loamy soil felt nourishing beneath their fingers, and the act of pushing their hands into it linked them to their ancestors who had tended these grounds long ago. As they worked, the sun dipped low in the sky, casting a golden hue over the landscape, and every Gevling felt a tingle of joy coursing through them. Returning to the plains was not just about finding a new home; it was about reclaiming their identity and reconnecting with the land that had sustained their people for generations. Each day spent rebuilding felt like stitching together a tapestry of their past, present, and future. As they looked out over the vast expanse of the plains, they felt gratitude swell in their hearts, and for the first time in a long while, they found themselves feeling complete and whole once again.

To try and win the hearts of the disgruntled members of the city, King Kedrick had ordered a monumental cleanup operation within Graigeth, restoring its former glory in a way that seemed almost miraculous. The once-dull walls, covered in layers of soot and grime from years of neglect and peril, sparkled anew, reflecting the sunlight like polished gems. It was as if the city had shed its old skin, emerging fresh and vibrant, ready to embrace the future with open arms. Every corner of Graigeth hummed with anticipation. The air, once heavy with the stench of smoke and decay, now carried the sweet scent of blooming flowers, mingled with the rich aromas of freshly baked bread and fragrant spices wafting from kitchens across the city. The streets were scrubbed clean and lined with colourful flags fluttering in the gentle breeze, beckoning citizens to step outside and celebrate.

Today was a historic day, a day to look forward, a day that embodied the promise of a brighter future for all of Graigeth and, indeed, all of Mantle, newly united in harmonious alliance. As the sun dipped lower in the sky, casting a warm golden glow over the restored city, a sense of renewal enveloped everyone. Today had been declared a bank holiday across Mantle, a joyful occasion to be known as Mantle Day, where hope blossomed like the flowers dotting the parks.

The End... for now!

# DIVERGENT MIND BOOKS

If you enjoyed this book, why not read one of the following fantasy books:


**Compilation** – A Collection of Short Stories
By David Peters
Kindle Price £1.99      Paperback Price £8.99
ISBN: 978-1-7394124-7-0


**The Life of Merlin**
By Harriet Davey
Paperback Price £6.99
ISBN: 978-1-7394124-3-2


Alternatively, why not read the memoir:


BROKEN – A NEVER ENDING JOURNEY
By Louise Bourdon
Paperback Price £12.99
ISBN: 978-1-7394124-5-6

# DIVERGENT MIND BOOKS ASSOCIATION

As an author, I've experienced the incredible power of storytelling. As someone diagnosed with autism later in life, I also understand the deep value of self-validation and having one's voice heard. This is why I publish my books with the valuable support of the Divergent Mind Books Association.

Their mission is to empower neurodivergent authors to share their stories with the world. They are doing this by providing low-cost ISBN numbers and free online courses to guide writers through their self-publishing journey.

Every book has the power to change a life. By supporting this association, you are helping to amplify neurodivergent voices, fostering a more inclusive society, and giving others the chance to achieve their goals and find their own sense of worth.

If you are interested, you can register for their free "Let's Write YOUR Book" online course by request, with your information to:

Divergentmindbooks@outlook.com

For more information, please visit the Association's website at www.divergentmindbooks.org.uk